Fritz spreads the paper ou[...] crowd around him. And t[...] middle of the front page of the *Los Angeles Times,* are pictures of Daddy and me and a headline that says:

TV STAR'S DAUGHTER MISSING

" 'Beverly Hills police have admitted that television star Michael McAllister's thirteen-year-old daughter, Kate, has been missing from his Beverly Hills home since early yesterday,' " Fritz reads out loud, " 'An investigation is now underway. As yet no ransom demand has been received, and there is speculation that the child's disappearance may be connected with a custody battle between McAllister and his ex-wife, Diana McAllister, who now lives in New York City and who has been unavailable for comment.' "

The *front page*. It feels like that nightmare I sometimes have of walking down the street naked with everybody staring at me. That's what it's like to be on the front page of a newspaper. Naked and embarrassing.

Also available from VAGABOND BOOKS

CAT-MAN'S DAUGHTER

by **Barbara Abercrombie**

Vagabond Books

SCHOLASTIC BOOK SERVICES
New York Toronto London Auckland Sydney Tokyo

For Gordon with love

ISBN 0-590-32727-5

12 11 10 9 8 7 6 5 4 3 2 1   3   3 4 5 6/8

1

The person I really want to see when I get off the plane in Los Angeles is Riley, my grandmother.

But there's Harry Thomas waiting to meet my flight, holding a dozen red roses and wearing all his silver-and-turquoise jewelry and weird sandals, and he's waving at me and yelling, "Kate!"

He helps me with the stuff I'm carrying (a tote bag with my glass animal collection wrapped up in Kleenex, the *Larousse Encyclopedia of the Animal World*, and the *Pictorial Encyclopedia of the Animal Kingdom*, plus the August issue of *Seventeen*) and whispers, "You know what happens when your father comes to the airport."

"What happens?"

"People go crazy. You know that. People just go crazy when they see Cat-Man in person."

"But isn't that what you want?"

"What?" Harry Thomas frowns.

"People going crazy when they see him. Isn't that what's supposed to happen?"

He keeps frowning. "Sure, but it's inconvenient. There could be a riot at the airport if everybody got excited about seeing Cat-Man."

When I was a little girl and first met Harry Thomas I thought his name was *Hairy* Thomas.

"You see what I mean?" he says.

"I guess so."

Sometimes I wish Daddy were a dentist or a truck driver or just sat behind a desk all day, instead of playing Cat-Man. It's okay for Harry Thomas, who's Daddy's agent and gets ten percent of all the money Daddy makes, and it's okay for Mom, who gets even more of the money and who doesn't seem to mind telling people that she used to be married to Cat-Man. But I find it embarrassing that my father jumps out of the bushes every Thursday night on ABC-TV in front of the whole country, pretending that two seconds ago he was a big, fluffy, black-and-white cat. This cat wanders around the neighborhood, in and out of houses, and whenever there's any trouble — a robbery or some kid having a problem — the cat is there listening and watching. Then he runs outside and disappears into the bushes, with drums and horns playing in the background, and then a few seconds later: Cat-Man! It's *that* kind of a show. I feel sorry for the cat.

On the freeway, driving toward Daddy's house in Beverly Hills, Harry says, "School going okay?"

"It's August."

2

"Right. Sure it is. How about camp? Didn't you go to camp for a while?"

"Yes."

"Did you like it?"

"No."

"Why not?"

"They melted the leftover Jell-O and pretended it was Kool-Aid. We had fourteen arts-and-crafts projects. And then everybody found out about my father. I've got requests for one hundred and eighty-two autographed pictures of Cat-Man."

"No problem. Give me the list and my secretary will send them out for you."

I'm still holding the roses; I wonder whose idea they were. Harry's secretary's? Daddy's? Harry clicks his rings on the steering wheel. I bet the roses were his idea. I like Harry a lot, even though he was the one who got Daddy the part of Cat-Man.

"Are you still married, Harry?" I ask.

He looks at me. "Why?"

"I was just wondering if you'd be interested in dating my mother."

"What is this? A joke?"

"No, I'm serious. I'm looking for somebody for my mother. Somebody I like."

"Well, I'm flattered, but —"

"I guess it's not a good idea. I don't think it would work out. You live in Los Angeles and she lives in New York, so it's doomed from the start."

"You're absolutely right," he says.

It's almost six o'clock in the evening — rush hour. My ears still buzz from the flight and I feel itchy and

3

hot in the dress Mom made me wear. It's got lace on the hem, which scratches my legs, and big droopy sleeves. I look like I could start flying if I flapped my arms hard enough. I hate dresses. The minute I get to Daddy's house I'm going to put on shorts and a T-shirt and go barefoot.

"How's Riley?" I ask.

"Don't know. She hasn't been around lately."

"Doesn't she know I'm here?"

"Don't think so. Your trip was kind of sudden."

Kind of sudden. I'm supposed to be at Shannon Rabb's slumber party on East 72nd Street in New York City right now, but here I am three thousand miles away, stuck in rush-hour traffic on the San Diego Freeway with Harry Thomas clicking his turquoise rings on his steering wheel.

Last night Daddy's lawyer called Mom's lawyer and said that Mom owed Daddy another week of me and that if I wasn't on a plane to California within twenty-four hours Mom would be arrested. My parents haven't spoken to each other since they were divorced — for two whole years. And that's why the lawyers have to handle everything. Mom has me most of the time and Daddy gets me on alternate Christmases, two-thirds of spring vacation, and four weeks every summer. This summer he had me only three weeks, but it took Daddy's lawyer shouting "Prison term!" over the phone to get Mom to put me on a plane today for that fourth week. I get bounced back and forth between New York and Los Angeles so much, I feel like a Ping-Pong ball.

Sometimes I think I should have my own lawyer. I could call up this lawyer of mine and say, "Hey,

4

get my father to New York for a couple of days. I want him to take me to some movies." And then my lawyer could tell Mom she'd be arrested (which seems to be the only way to get her attention these days) if she didn't start talking to Daddy.

Harry turns off the freeway onto Wilshire Boulevard. "Your father's glad you're here. So's Jessica."

"Jessica?"

"Didn't you meet her last month?"

"The one who does nail-polish commercials?"

"No, that was Agatha. Jessica was answering fan mail. Blond. Cute."

I know exactly what she's going to look like. Daddy has Barbie-doll taste in girl friends. They're always young and cute, and none of them ever looks like Mom, who even though she's very skinny could nail a mugger with a dirty look. And the Barbie dolls never ever sound like Mom, who has been known to talk for an hour or more, not only without stopping but apparently without even breathing.

What I want to do is find Daddy a really terrific girl friend, preferably an older lady who doesn't want to start having babies and who will be a good stepmother to me. And I'm working on finding Mom a good husband. Right now she's going with a real dud named Chad. She thinks he's sexy. I think he's got adenoid problems: He talks through his nose. I'm considering divorcing Mom if she decides to marry him.

"I don't think I met Jessica," I say to Harry.

"Hello, Katykins!" Daddy gives me a big bear hug. He smells of special shaving lotion, limes and spices, and his shirt smells clean and just ironed. He looks like he's in his twenties instead of almost forty. He has lots of dark, wiry hair that he's always brushing out of his eyes. My mother's parents have a thing about hair. Nobody on my mother's side of the family has thick hair, and whenever my Florida grandmother comes to New York for a visit she always says, "Well, there was one thing about Michael. He did have lovely hair."

Daddy holds me at arm's length and grins at me. "Look at you! You've grown again. You've grown about a foot since last month." He and Jessica look at me as though I'm that vine that grows so fast in Georgia — kudzu. We studied it in school. It grows right in front of your eyes, two feet overnight.

Then Jessica gives me one of those kisses that isn't really a kiss, just sort of a cool brush of her cheek against mine. She's got golden hair that looks like it's just been washed and skin that's never known a zit, and she must be all of twenty years old. Seven years older than I am.

I feel spotted and about six feet tall. I don't know what to do with my hands. If I have pockets I usually stick my hands in them, but this dress my mother thinks is so charming doesn't have any pockets.

Daddy leans against the banister, and Jessica slouches with one hip out like a fashion model. We're standing in the front hallway like we've just met at a party. The house stretches out around us, cool and quiet. Everything in it is too clean: white carpets that look like nobody ever walks on them,

6

white walls — you can tell instantly that no kids or animals live in this house.

"Well," says Daddy and picks up my suitcase, "let's get you settled." Jessica takes my tote bag, and I carry the roses and my books as the three of us go upstairs.

It's a little like *The Twilight Zone*. My bedroom in Daddy's house is exactly the same as my bedroom in Mom's apartment. The same four-poster bed with a white canopy and five teddy bears lined up against the pillows. The same yellow rug and striped yellow-and-white wallpaper and the bookcase filled with the same set of *Britannica Junior Encyclopaedia*. The only difference is that the pictures on my bedside table in New York are of Mom, and here they're of Daddy. And there's a different phone number on the telephone and a three-hour time difference on the white digital clock.

Mom did it all long distance from New York. The first time I came out here and saw it I called her right up on the phone.

"Weren't you *surprised*?" she asked in her cracky voice that sounds like she has terminal laryngitis. "Doesn't it make you feel *secure*?"

"What it makes me feel is that I never left New York. It's creepy!"

"Dr. Ludlow said it would blunt the adjustment period for you. He said it would give you a feeling of security."

"Were Dr. Ludlow's parents divorced?"

That stopped her for a minute.

"I mean, what makes him an expert on *me*?" I asked.

7

"I should go to jail for wanting you to be a happy, secure person? It's a terrific bedroom! I just want you to be happy. I'm not trying to be mean."

"I know, Mom."

"Look, you're going to like it once you get used to it. If your father has to drag you back there all the time you might as well feel comfortable!"

"Feel comfortable? Does a Ping-Pong ball ever feel comfortable?"

"What do Ping-Pong balls have to do with it?"

Nobody understands any of this except my grandmother. Riley knows that these identical bedrooms aren't going to solve anything; not with my parents fighting over me like I'm some sort of prize.

All I want is a family again. Like my friend Shannon's, for instance. Her parents love each other and kiss and hug a lot without being embarrassing about it, and she's got a younger brother who once in a while does something really lousy like sell pages of her diary at school, but basically he's not so bad. When you're at Shannon's you don't have to pretend anything, you can just be yourself and everybody loves you.

I know my family will never be like Shannon's, but I'm counting on stepparents. Two sort-of-normal families might add up to one normal family.

"Christina will come up and help you unpack in a few minutes," says Daddy, putting my suitcase on the chest at the foot of the bed. "How was your flight, baby?"

"It was okay." I take my glass animals out of the tote bag and start setting them out on top of my dresser.

"How's your mother doing these days?" He says "your mother" like it's some kind of a disease. As if he's asking, "How's tuberculosis doing these days?"

"She's about the same, I guess." Which is my standard diplomatic answer when they ask me about each other. It's like being a politician. You've got to say the right thing all the time or everybody goes crazy. I make a circle out of my glass animals — the rabbit family, the mama cat with her three kittens, the three deer, the mouse family, and the little yellow ducks. "How's Riley?"

"Oh, Riley. You know Riley."

He smiles his best Cat-Man smile at me. I smile my Daughter-of-Cat-Man smile right back. I know Riley, but does *he*? I don't think he appreciates his own mother.

"When can I see her?"

He turns to Jessica, who says, "I think it's scheduled for Friday."

Most people would say, Let's jump in the car and drive down to San Pedro to see your grandmother, if that's what you want to do. But not at Daddy's house. For the whole two years since my parents' divorce, my visits have been scheduled like military operations. When I was here last month, Daddy had me so scheduled I only got to see Riley twice.

"The Museum of Natural History and rose garden in Exhibition Park tomorrow," Jessica is saying, "Magic Mountain on Wednesday, Knott's Berry Farm on Thursday, and Friday Marineland and your grandmother."

I know more about Los Angeles than any person alive because every time I visit, Daddy's current girl friend takes me to all the tourist attractions to impress him with her interest in me.

"Well!" says Daddy, then doesn't seem to know what else to say. I don't know what to say either. Maybe I'd think of something if Jessica weren't hanging on his arm like she owned him. Sometimes I think I miss Daddy more when I'm *with* him than when I'm in New York.

He pats my shoulder. "People are coming over for dinner —"

"Oh." I try not to look disappointed.

"I'm sorry, Katie, we couldn't get out of it. We'll leave you alone so you can change."

Change. That makes we feel like I'm supposed to turn into somebody else. I mean, *change.*

He pauses in the doorway with Jessica. "You okay?"

"Yes."

"Sure?" He smiles at me. "One-hundred-percent sure?"

"Sure."

"What's wrong, Katie?"

"I want to see Riley."

"You can see Riley. No big deal. You're seeing her Friday — what time Friday, Jessica?"

"Around three in the afternoon, I think."

"Friday afternoon. That isn't forever, is it?"

"I don't want to wait until Friday."

He makes a noise through his teeth. "Look, we'll talk about it, okay? We'll juggle the schedule if that's what you want."

I can hear them whispering as they go down the hall, probably discussing what to do about the Kate

10

"situation." That's what my mother's boyfriend Chad always calls any kind of a problem. "Bunny, what's the olive situation around here?" he'll say if he can't find any for his martini. Her real name is Diana but he calls her Bunny.

Bunny and Cat-Man. Instead of a mother and father I've got Bunny and Cat-Man.

I sit on my bed in the same room I just left and wait for Christina, Daddy's housekeeper, to come up. The house feels like it's melting away and I'm in a yellow-and-white bedroom just floating through space, unattached to a house or a city or a family. Just floating around in space all by myself.

2

"**H**ow's Riley?" I ask Christina first thing.

"Riley's fine," she says, hugging me. "It's you we worry about, Katie. How are *you?*"

"Lousy."

"Lousy?" Christina clutches her pillowy front like I've stabbed her. She always takes me very seriously.

"Well, I'm not dying or anything."

"Oh, poor little Katie. It's not right for you to be pulled back and forth between the two of them." And then suddenly she smiles at me. She looks like one of those old-fashioned dolls with fine, pale hair and bright eyes and pink cheeks. "Don't worry."

"Don't worry?"

"Don't worry. Don't feel lousy," she says firmly, beaming like she's got a light inside of her. She puts

12

the roses Harry Thomas gave me in a vase on my bedside table.

I open my suitcase and start to unpack. "You know what's wrong with me?"

"What?"

"My plan isn't working. Riley always says you can't drift. You've got to have a plan to get through life."

Christina puts a stack of my bikini underpants and 32AA bras in the dresser drawer. "What's this plan that's not working?"

"Finding the right husband for my mother and the right wife for my father."

"No wonder you're having problems! That's a complicated plan."

"You're telling me? I even asked Harry Thomas if he'd be interested."

"Katie!"

"Oh, I didn't ask him if he wanted to marry her. I'm subtle about it. I just asked him if he'd be interested in dating her. He thought I was kidding; they always do. A really terrific carpenter came to build new bookshelves a few months ago — he showed me how to make miniature furniture out of scraps of wood — but he thought it was a joke, too. Mom said she'd kill me if I tried to fix her up with a date one more time."

Christina unpacks my T-shirts and shorts, looking like she's swallowed about a dozen canaries.

"Christina?"

"Yes, Katie?"

"How's everything with you?"

"Fine." She smiles.

"I mean, you seem so happy about something —"

"Well, of course. I'm happy to see you."

"Oh."

Christina has cooked and kept house for Daddy ever since the divorce. Riley discovered her when Christina sold her a pound of fudge at See's Candy, and when Riley found out Christina plays the flute, she convinced her that she'd have more time to practice if she came here to work. I think Riley really wanted to make sure there'd be someone responsible to look after Daddy.

As Christina and I finish unpacking my suitcase, she hums a tune she plays a lot on her flute. Why can't Daddy fall in love with someone like Christina?

"I'm afraid Kate has jet lag," says Jessica.

Eight grown-ups look at me as if jet lag shows like poison ivy or leprosy. I scratch my arm and wish I could think of something interesting to say. Or *anything* to say. But I can't, so I just keep on eating. Christina has fixed Cornish game hens that look like tiny dead birds on everyone's plate, so I concentrate on my artichoke, which requires a lot of attention.

"I haven't had jet lag in sixteen years," says a man whose shirt is unbuttoned practically down to his belly button.

"When I went to Africa last summer I couldn't move for three days," says Honey Blackstone, who plays the the owner of the cat on *Cat-Man*. At one time Honey was at the top of my list for possible stepmothers, but when I discussed it with her she said she wouldn't marry an actor if her life depended on it; especially an actor who was twenty years younger than she was.

"Hilary breaks out in hives if there's more than a two-hour time difference."

"Hilary would."

Daddy is leaning toward the woman in red silk overalls on his right, listening like his life depends on whatever she's saying. It's kind of a trick actors have. They're professional listeners. I wonder what my life would be like if he weren't an actor. It's very weird to be an actor's kid.

When Christina clears away the dinner plates, I ask, "May I be excused, please?"

"No dessert, Katie?" asks Daddy.

I shake my head.

"I'll go up with you," says Jessica.

When we're out in the hallway I can hear everybody back in the dining room buzzing with comments. "Isn't she *darling*." "Hasn't she grown." "Looks so much like you." What else can they say? Poor kid never opened her mouth. She'll turn into a freak if she gets any taller. Too bad her face is breaking out. Thirteen and no bosom.

"I thought we'd leave at ten tomorrow morning," says Jessica as we go upstairs. "Your father said you really like the Natural History Museum."

"Yes."

"I've never been there."

"I'll show you around," I say. "It's a very interesting place."

"Really?"

15

"Yes." We walk down the hall toward my room. "If you like animals and nature and stuff like that."

"Oh, I do," says Jessica, all whispery and pink. "I really do."

"I'll loan you my animal encyclopedias if you'd like to look them over tonight. Sort of study up the the museum."

"Thank you."

I can tell her heart's not in it.

"I have a surprise for you tomorrow," she says. "A friend."

"A friend?" What's she talking about? All my old friends are in Santa Monica, where we used to live before the divorce, and all my new friends are in New York. "What friend?"

"You don't know her yet, but she's your age."

Why do grown-ups always think that just because somebody's your age you'll automatically be friends? There are a lot of people my exact same age I can't stand, let alone be friends with.

"Doesn't that sound like fun?" She turns on the lights in my room.

"I guess so." I wish she'd just relax and stop auditioning for the part of stepmother. I hand her the animal encyclopedias.

"Do you need anything?" she asks, standing in the doorway, sort of sagging. Those encyclopedias are heavy.

"I'm fine."

"If you need anything, you know how to ring for Christina, don't you?"

"Sure." I'm beginning to catch on to the fact that Jessica has moved in. Which I really don't want to think about in too much detail. At least Chad hasn't moved into our apartment in New York. Not while I'm there anyway. When I got back from camp I found one of his socks in the laundry. Mom said it was definitely not Chad's sock and must belong to the maid. I've never seen the maid wear maroon socks, but I dropped the subject.

Jessica gives me one of her little cheek-brushing kisses and says good night. After she's gone, her perfume hangs heavy and sweet in my room. I can almost taste it.

What if they get married? What if they have a baby? A whole bunch of babies? What exactly would be my position around here? Older stepsister? Old child from former marriage?

I put my pajamas on and brush my teeth. I've got to talk to Riley. She's the only person I can really trust; she's never let me down.

Two years ago Mom, very serious and teary, came into my room in our old house to tell me she and Daddy were getting a divorce. "This won't change *your* life, Kate," she said to me. "This is between your father and me. We both love you very much. The divorce doesn't concern you."

Didn't concern me?

When I called up Riley to tell her what was going on, she said. "A divorce won't change your life? Who are they trying to kid? Happy endings belong to fairy tales. Of course it's going to change your life! It's going to be awful for a while, Katie, but at least it can't get much worse."

She was wrong. It got worse. At least they were still speaking to each other at first and trying to decide what would be best for me. That was before Mom and I moved to New York, and Dr. Ludlow came on the scene with his security syndromes, and the Barbie dolls started answering the phone at Daddy's new house. Then my parents got so mad at each other it seemed to spread like chicken pox or the measles or something. Pretty soon they were mad at everybody, and that's when they stopped speaking to each other.

I pick up the phone next to my bed and dial Riley's number. Fritz answers. Fritz is even older than Riley, and a long, long time ago he used to be a sailor. Riley's house is always filled with people who don't have any other place to go. Sometimes they stay a few weeks, sometimes for years. Some of them never leave, like Fritz.

"Fritz! It's me — Katie."

"Hello, Katie! Where are you?"

"Here. In Beverly Hills. My father was going to have my mother arrested if I didn't come out right away. So here I am."

"We heard all about it. Didn't know when you'd get here, though."

"May I speak to Riley please?"

"Riley and Myra went to the movies. I'll have her call you back when she gets in if it's not too late."

"Okay, Fritz. Give everybody my love." I hang up

feeling a lot better. Once Riley told me if things didn't get better with my parents she'd think of a plan to help me. And Riley usually has a lot better luck with her plans than I have with mine.

3

My clock says six-fifteen, but I'm awake because six-fifteen in California is nine-fifteen in New York, and I'm still on New York time. It's already very hot and the sun is just coming up. The sky outside my window has streaks of pink feathery clouds. We're having a Santa Ana, which is a hot, dry wind that blows off the desert.

Riley never called back last night. I pick up my bedside phone and call her. She'll be awake; everybody always gets up early at Riley's house. But nobody answers. The phone rings. Then there's a click for the automatic answering service, and Riley's recorded voice is saying, "Thank you for calling Birthday Business. There is no one in the office right now, but if you will leave your name and number at the sound of the beep, Birthday Business will return your call. Thank you very much."

I hate talking to answering machines. It's like talking to a wall. There's the sound of the beep and I say, "Hi, Riley." The machine whirs, waiting for me to say something interesting. "This is Kate. Where are you? Please call me." I hang up.

Six-twenty. Where could she be? Where could a whole houseful of people be at six-twenty in the morning?

The door handle of the car gives me a shock. It's so dry and hot out my lips are chapping.

"Do you have any Chap Stick?" I ask.

"No. Do you want me to stop at a drugstore and buy some?"

"No, that's okay."

Jessica's jeans are so tight I wonder how she can get behind the wheel and into a sitting position. What are we going to talk about all day? Her hands are small and perfect-looking like the rest of her, except for one thing: She bites her nails. Right down to the quick, just like I do. Jessica's biting her nails makes me like her a little bit.

The air smells of smoke and cars. You can actually see the heat shimmering off the freeway. So many cars — where's everybody going?

"I hate driving on the freeway," says Jessica. "I never even saw a freeway until I was fifteen years old."

"I was practically born on one."

"What do you mean?"

"My father got into a traffic jam when he was taking my mother to the hospital. She still talks about it. She says she told him to take Santa Monica

21

Boulevard but he never listened to her about anything."

"Hmm," says Jessica. She concentrates on driving. I look out the window. Sometimes when you don't know what to talk about, it's better just not to say anything.

Next to the Museum of Natural History there's an enormous rose garden that looks like waves of bright colors from a distance. The roses are all tagged with their names — "Sutter's Gold," "Floribunda Bon-Bon," "Razzle-Dazzle," "Blaze." I love the names almost as much as I love the roses.

"Bees," says Jessica.

"Where?"

"Everywhere. All around the roses. I'm allergic to bee stings. I mean, really allergic. I can get very sick if a bee stings me and I don't have my medicine."

"Well, do you have your medicine?"

"No."

"You should always have it with you." I feel older than Jessica instead of seven years younger. I've got to find my father a nice middle-aged lady with a lot of sense who will take care of us.

Inside the museum it's cool, and the smells are old and dry and mysterious. Except for the basement floor, where the cafeteria is, which smells of hot dogs and tomato sauce. Jessica's heels go *clickety-clickety* on the stone floors. My sneakers go *schlup-schlup*.

We start with the Hall of Exotic Mammals, on the second floor. The first time I came here I was five years old and Riley brought me. Riley has a theory

22

that animals live much more honest lives than people, and that human beings better start paying attention. So we've spent a lot of time here. Riley wears sneakers, too.

The animals are the real thing: stuffed and looking just like they do in the wild, surrounded by all the plants and birds and insects and scenery of their natural habitat. You can even get an idea of how the animal usually feels — whether it's curious or shy or nervous or bold.

This might sound creepy, to have a dead animal stuffed and looking shy or nervous or bold, but it isn't. It's actually so interesting that you don't think about it being dead and stuffed. You think about how it got along in life, what it ate, where it lived, and how it lived. Like Riley says, it makes you realize how simple and sensible life can be.

The hall is dim and the habitat groups are lit like little windows. Voices echo even when you whisper.

"You're really going to like Natalie," says Jessica, frowning at a honey badger who's gobbling up honey and covered with bees.

"Who's Natalie?" I ask as we quickly move on to the aardvarks.

"Natalie Blanchard. The friend you're going to meet after we leave this place."

I wish Jessica would stop taking it for granted that this person my age is going to be my friend.

"Her new father directed some episodes of *Cat-Man*," says Jessica, wrinkling her nose at a warthog who has warty bumps all over his snout.

"New father?" I repeat. That term makes me very

nervous. As if fathers can be traded around like used cars or furniture. I don't want a *new* father. I want my father plus *another* father — a backup father for New York.

We come to the giant red kangaroos. "Males grow to be six feet tall and often box with one another," I read out loud.

"Hmm," says Jessica. "They just bought a new home. I hear it's fabulous."

Riley loves the red kangaroos. She says they know how to box with dignity and grace. I miss Riley more than ever, being in our favorite place. Why didn't she call me back? *Where* is she?

Jessica yawns and limps slightly. We leave the exotic mammals and go into the Hall of North American Mammals. In the first habitat three adult musk oxen stand in snow with a baby musk ox.

"Oh, doesn't that snow look marvelous," says Jessica.

"It's not real snow," I say.

"Well, no, but it looks like snow. It's supposed to be snow."

"It's soap."

"Soap?"

"Tide. They have this deal with the Tide company. They order two hundred tons of Tide at a time."

I don't have the faintest idea what they use for snow, but I feel like bugging Jessica. I don't know why I feel so mean and antsy. Jessica's not so bad, and at least she's trying. She's just awfully young. If only I could talk to Riley, everything would be all right.

Jessica moves along to the mountain goats with their spiky little horns and white fuzzy coats. "They live in bands; family life is not well defined," says the sign. Welcome to the club.

"They just got married last month," says Jessica.

"What?"

"Natalie's mother and Derek."

It's pretty obvious to me that Jessica doesn't feel she can learn anything from animals. I don't think she even likes animals — which is one of my first tests for a possible future stepmother.

"Someday I'm going to have a mountain goat as a pet," I tell her.

"You're kidding."

"No, I'm not. My father says I can have any kind of pet I want. I'm going to fill up the whole house with really weird wild animals. Some of them might not even be housebroken." Is she getting the picture? This will definitely not be the home of Jessica's dreams.

Sea lions, bison, cougars, and coyotes. "Coyotes generally mate for life. The male is a good husband, defending, providing for, and helping train the pups." Even coyotes have normal families.

"Oh, how cute they are," says Jessica.

"Do you want to see the African mammals?" I ask, but my heart isn't in it.

"Didn't we just see them?"

"No, those were exotic mammals."

"What's the difference?" Jessica sits down on a bench at the end of the hall, and slides off her high heels. "Oh, my feet hurt."

"You should wear flats. Or sneakers, like I do."

"Your father hates flats." She looks at my feet and says quickly, "But on you it's different. I mean, he likes you in sneakers . . ." Her voice trails off.

"You'd never see an animal wearing high heels," I say so loudly that some people looking at the habitats turn around and stare at me.

Jessica looks at me with a little frown. "Well, no."

"They've got too much sense."

She just frowns and looks confused. Finally she looks at her watch. "We're due at Natalie's house in fifteen minutes."

"Let's go," I say.

4

Natalie Blanchard's favorite expression is "the pits."

"This house is the pits," she says, balancing her Birkenstock sandals on her toes. Then she drops the sandals into the thick carpet and puts her bare feet on the glass coffee table. "You know what Adelle put in my room?"

"Adelle?" I ask.

"My mother. She put a stage in my room."

"A *stage*?"

"As in theatrical."

"You give plays up there?"

"No, no. I *dance* on it."

"You give dances in your room?"

"*Oh,*" says Natalie, and looks up at the ceiling. "I don't *give* dances on it. I dance on it. Or I'm sup-

27

posed to. I take tap-dancing lessons. I'm supposed to tap-dance on it. But I never do. Have you ever tap-danced on a stage in your bedroom all by yourself?"

"No."

"It's the pits," says Natalie.

Besides the sandals (which look like little leather canoes) Natalie Blanchard is wearing a Danskin top (which reveals she has the second flattest chest in the United States of America), a long cotton skirt that hangs just above her ankles, and a green scarf tied around her head gypsy style. From under the scarf two silver earrings dangle down, and about a yard of dark, frizzy hair bursts out in all directions.

"You want to see it?" she asks.

"Sure."

"I'll show you the fish, too." She slides her feet into the leather canoes and clomps out of the room. I hurry after her.

"Fish?"

"My fish. I keep fish."

Natalie's new house is even bigger than my father's house. I follow her down hallways and up a big staircase, then through more hallways until we finally reach her room. It's like a cave. The shutters are closed and the only light comes from about a dozen glowing, bubbling aquariums lined up against one wall. In a dim corner I can see the stage. Clothes are hanging on chairs and doorknobs, and there are shoes, books, and games scattered all over the floor. The air conditioning is turned up so high that it's chilly.

"These are the guppies." Natalie kneels down in front of one of the aquariums, her face faintly green in the reflected light. "You can watch the mothers having babies. They don't lay eggs. They're like people. The babies pop right out of their bodies. The mothers are the big colorless ones. The males are the flashy ones. I have a special tank for the mother guppies because everybody eats the babies if they're born in the big tank. Even the mothers eat them. Guppies are not noted for brains and maternal feelings."

Natalie talks like a machine gun. *Rata-tat-tat.*

"Those are the angelfish in that tank," she says as I drift down the line of tanks. "They sulk if the water isn't right or if they don't like the food. That's Carl the Catfish down at the bottom. He cleans. He's four years old. I got him for a present on my ninth birthday. We were living —" She pauses for a moment and thinks. "We were living in the Hollywood hills then. That was just before we moved to Malibu."

"You move around a lot, don't you?"

"Is the Pope Catholic?" She gets up to open the shutters, and we both blink in the sudden bright light. I look out at Natalie's mother and Jessica rubbing oil on their legs and drinking wine by the pool.

"When you move, how do you move all the fish and stuff?" I ask, sitting down on the stage.

"I put the fish in those plastic cups with the tops, from McDonald's. The last move took sixty-two cups. I make my mother take the tanks in the car so they don't get cracked by the movers."

"That must be quite a job."

29

She shrugs her pale, bony shoulders and suddenly looks bored with the whole discussion. "See, it has a curtain even," she says, pointing to the side of the stage.

"Have you had it long?"

"Three months. Since we moved in after Adelle married Derek. It's built in." Natalie kicks off her sandals and sits in the middle of her bed. She reaches down to peel some dark red polish off her big toenail. "My friend Julie can bite her toenails. Can you?"

"No."

"Neither can I. You have to be very limber. Julie takes ballet. Anyway, before Adelle married Derek, we lived about a mile from here, right off Sunset, with Jason."

"Who's Jason?"

"A drip. A verified turkey. He wore six gold chains around his neck, and he used to dye the hair on his chest. I caught him doing it once. He used Clairol's Bashful Brown. Adelle married him about three years after she and Jeffrey were divorced."

"Jeffrey?"

"My father. Who now lives in San Diego. Anyway, Jason had five boys. Each one was a turkey. They were all cousins of Derek's first wife's kids. Did you ever notice that everybody in Beverly Hills is related? Do you have any brothers or sisters?"

"No."

"Too bad. I have a brother. His name is Dwight."

"Does he live here?"

"No." Natalie starts on the polish on her other big toenail.

"Where does he live?"

"In San Diego with Jeffrey and his new wife. I mean Jeffrey's new wife, not Dwight's. Dwight's a little boy. He's eight."

"Do you see him often?"

"No."

"Never?"

"Just during spring vacation. My parents made this deal — she got me and he got Dwight."

"That's awful."

"The pits," says Natalie. "I think Adelle secretly feels she got the bad end of the deal." She looks up from her toes and stares at me for a while, then finally says, "Can you keep secrets?"

"Sure, I can keep secrets."

"Hmm." She doesn't look convinced. She tugs on her silver earrings and continues to stare at me.

I wonder if Natalie Blanchard is a genuine crazy person. I always think I'm crazy, but maybe she's the real thing.

"I have this grandmother —" I start to say.

"Yeah?" says Natalie, sweeping little shreds of red polish off her bed and onto the carpet. "So what? I've got half a dozen."

"Well, you wanted to know about brothers and sisters and family. My closest family member is my grandmother. She's one of my best friends. She lives in San Pedro."

"Nobody lives in San Pedro," says Natalie.

"Why do you say something like that?"

"Why not?"

"*Thousands* of people live in San Pedro."

"None of them are in the business."

"There are other businesses besides movies and television, you know. As a matter of fact, Riley, my grandmother, happens to have her own business."

"What kind?"

"It's called Birthday Business."

"*Birthday* Business?" says Natalie with a little sneer. "What do they do?"

"They cater birthday parties for kids. Riley gives a puppet show, and Fritz bakes the cake —"

"Fritz? Who's Fritz?"

"He used to be in the merchant marine. He was a sailor and did all the baking on the ship. Now he cooks for everybody at Riley's house. He's almost seventy-five."

"Almost seventy-five what?"

"Years. He's almost seventy-five years old."

"And he's baking birthday cakes for little kids?"

"Why not?" I say.

She gives me one of her bony shrugs.

"And there's Hank," I go on. "He's five years old and he's in charge of balloons and general clean-up —"

"Wait a minute." Natalie holds up her hand. "A five-year-old kid? Where did he come from?"

"He's a long story." I rearrange myself on the hard wooden stage.

"How long can it be?" says Natalie. "He's five years old."

"Well, his mother ran away from home when she was sixteen — I think she lived in Oregon or some-place like that — anyway, she came to Los Angeles to be a rock star but instead she ended up at Riley's house where she had Hank. Then she ran away again and no one has seen her since."

"Is that your idea of a long story?"

"I cut out a lot of details."

"So who else is there?"

"There's Myra — she used to be a governess, but when the girls she took care of grew up, she was sent away and had a nervous breakdown —"

"A real nervous breakdown?" asks Natalie.

"I guess so. That's what everybody called it."

"Go on. Who else?"

"Well, there's Austin —"

"Austin? What kind of a name is Austin?"

"It suits him, actually. I don't know why, it just does."

"What does he do?"

"He's an artist. Half of Riley's attic is his studio. He takes the photographs at the birthday parties."

"This is interesting," says Natalie. "Basically most things bore me. But this interests me. How does your grandmother find all these people? How do they find *her*?"

"Different ways. Hank's mother fainted in front of her on an escalator at a department store. I think it was the May Company. And Fritz — she met him in a park in San Pedro. Riley always talks to strangers. She says that they're usually more interesting than people you know, because people you know, you know all about anyway."

"That makes sense."

"I'm not sure where she met Austin. She met Myra at a Dodgers game."

"Does anyone ever leave?"

"Oh, sure, but then other people come and take their places."

"Do you have a job with this Birthday Business?"

"No, I'm not there often enough. I used to spend whole summers there before my parents got divorced, but she didn't have the business then. And now I'm not there very much. It's kind of complicated."

"Complicated!" says Natalie and jumps off the bed. "You don't know what complicated is until you live with Adelle!" She bends down and touches her toes. "This grandmother of yours — Riley — where does she live in San Pedro?"

"Near the harbor. One-twenty-one Ocean Avenue."

Natalie's eyes narrow to little slits in her white face. "Maybe I'll stop by on my way to see Dwight."

"I thought you only saw him during spring vacation."

She comes over to me and grabs my wrist so hard I think her fingers are going to go right through the skin. "I'm running away," she says. "And if you tell anybody I'll *kill you*."

She's so crazy I believe her. I rub my wrist. "When are you leaving?"

"Soon. *Don't tell.*"

"Don't worry, I won't."

"I've got this very carefully planned. I don't want anybody to screw it up."

"Look, I'm not going to tell anybody."

Natalie goes over to the aquariums and feeds the

fish from a can of tropical-fish food. Finally she says, "You want to go for a swim?"

For one tiny instant I think she means in the aquarium.

"I didn't bring a suit," I say.

"You can borrow one. We've got extras in the pool house."

We go downstairs without speaking. I'm trying to imagine Natalie showing up at Riley's house on her way to San Diego. Somehow I can't imagine Natalie anywhere except in this big fancy house with all the fish tanks and long hallways.

The air outside is so dry and sudden that it catches at the back of my throat. We both squint in the white, hot light on the patio. Natalie's mother and Jessica wave to us from the pool. Jessica looks a lot happier here than she did in the Hall of Exotic Mammals.

"Did you offer your guest a snack?" calls Natalie's mother. She's very tan and thin and wears sunglasses so big they look like goggles.

"Your guest wasn't hungry," Natalie calls back.

"What did you say?"

"I said, 'Your guest wasn't hungry.' "

"Your what?"

"Your guest. My guest."

"Natalie, are you trying to be funny?"

"Her name is Kate!"

Natalie's mother has this look on her face as if what she really wants to do is strangle Natalie. "I *know* what your guest's name is. Don't get smart with me, Natalie."

35

"La-de-da," says Natalie under her breath as we head for the pool house.

"You hear me, Natalie?" yells her mother.

"I've got ears!" Natalie yells back.

"My mother's a very nervous person," she says when we're inside putting on bathing suits. "She's insecure. Is your father going to marry Jessica?"

"I don't know. I'm trying to find him somebody older and more mature. Jessica's too young for him."

When we're in the pool Natalie says, "*Cat-Man*'s a dumb show, but I like your father. What's he like?"

"Well, he's —" What *is* he like? "He can be very funny sometimes. Not funny like you can tell about it later and it's still funny — but it's funny and unexpected at the time. If you know what I mean. He *was* like that anyway — but lately he's gotten pretty serious. He's changed a lot, I guess. I don't see him that much anymore. He's usually working when I'm out here."

Natalie floats on her back, her eyes closed. "But at least you see him. You're staying in the same house. My father makes an official visit to see me once a year. My mother won't let him come to the house, so we meet in a restaurant and I have to go there in a taxi. And then Jeffrey and I just sit and try to think of stuff to talk about. Really a gala occasion. Then I go down to San Diego for a week in April."

"Doesn't your mother ever see your little brother?"

"No. He was so young when they got a divorce they decided it would be easier if he just thought of his stepmother as his real mother, even though he knows she's not. You know who it's easier for — my parents. Not Dwight. And what Dwight thinks is that Adelle doesn't love him. I tell him that's not true, but he's no dummy." Natalie's talking very softly so her mother and Jessica can't hear. "He gets into a lot of trouble for an eight-year-old kid. That's why I'm going to move down there to look after him. This isn't just another runaway. I'm leaving for good."

"What's your mother going to say?"

"She probably won't notice."

"Come on, Natalie."

"Okay, so she'll notice. She'll notice and be relieved."

"Natalie — let me give you a piece of advice."

She rolls over and treads water, her hair everywhere and her hands fanning the water. She looks like one of her fish. "What advice?"

"Don't go around telling strangers you're planning to run away. Somebody will tell and screw it up for you."

"I don't tell strangers."

"You told me."

She gives me this look, as if she could chew up iron nails and swallow them. "You're not a stranger."

"What am I then?"

"I'm not sure yet," she says, and dives under the water.

5

"**H**as Riley called?" I ask Christina the minute we get home. She's in the kitchen playing her flute; I hate to interrupt her, but I'm beginning to feel desperate about Riley. Christina shakes her head. "Are you sure?"

She nods. Her gauzy yellow dress floats around her in layers, and even though she's playing the flute, she seems to be smiling.

"Maybe she called when you were out," I suggest.

She puts the silver flute down on the table. "I wasn't out. And if I'd been out, the service would have answered."

"That's true. Did you check the service?"

"I didn't have to. I wasn't out."

"Well, why hasn't Riley called me back? Where was everybody this morning?"

Christina just smiles and says, "We're having spaghetti for dinner tonight."

"Well," I say as I pick up the phone, "somebody's got to answer sometime today."

Somebody does after the second ring but doesn't say anything.

"Hello?" I say.

"Hello," says a small voice. It's Hank.

"Hank, this is Kate. Is Riley there?"

"Hello, hello!"

"Listen, Hank, what's going on? Do you know where Riley is?"

"Riley?" He's shouting as if he's in Europe and we've got a bad connection.

"Yes, *Riley*."

"Hank!" cries Hank.

"Is Fritz there?" Now I'm yelling, too. "Let me talk to Fritz, Hank!"

"Not Fritz, *Hank*."

I'm losing track of this whole conversation. "Hello, Hank," I shout back. "Can you hear me?"

"Good-bye!" Hank says and hangs up.

I dial again and after five rings there's a click, and then Riley's recorded voice says, "Thank you for calling Birthday Business. There is no one in the office right now, but if you will leave your name . . ."

"Did you have a good day, Katie?" asks Daddy at dinner. Here we are, a typical family of Beverly Hills. Daddy, old child from former marriage, and Daddy's friend. We're eating out on the patio where the air smells of flowers. We can hear the wind in the trees; the candles flicker.

"Oh, she had a super time, didn't you, Kate?" says Jessica. She's got her hair pinned up on top of her head with white flowers stuck in it. "Natalie's darling, don't you think so? And their home! Michael, it's fabulous. They're putting in a tennis court."

"Derek's crazy," says Daddy, finishing his salad. "He's supporting six kids and three ex-wives. What's Adelle like?"

"Very nice." Jessica plays with the flower in her hair. "A little tense, but nice."

Christina clears the salad plates, then serves the spaghetti. She always fixes my favorite food when I'm here.

"That's a lovely dress you're wearing, Christina," says Jessica.

Christina just smiles and floats out, looking like she's swallowed another batch of canaries.

Daddy covers his spaghetti with Parmesan cheese. "What's up tomorrow?" There are little tired lines around his eyes. He's wearing a blue cotton shirt that matches his eyes. I wish Jessica weren't here so I could talk to him. Really talk to him instead of talking *around* things all the time. That's what normal families do — talk, say what's on their minds. They don't have to worry they might say the wrong thing and somebody will get mad and stop talking or go out and hire a lawyer.

"We're going to Magic Mountain," says Jessica. "You like Magic Mountain, don't you, Katie?"

"Well, if she doesn't we could go somewhere else.

40

Would you rather go to Disneyland, Kate?"

I twirl a forkful of spaghetti around on my plate. I've been to Disneyland thirty-eight times. How can you feel sorry for yourself for going to Disneyland thirty-eight times? With probably about a million kids in this country who are dying to go to Disneyland, I not only feel sorry for myself, I feel guilty about feeling sorry for myself.

"You know what? It's going to be hot again tomorrow; why don't you two go to the beach?" He reaches across the table and pats my hand. "Remember, Katie? We used to go to the beach every weekend in Santa Monica."

"Well, I thought —" Jessica gets very antsy whenever the past is brought up. That's another thing — a really good stepmother will have been married before, so she won't be so jealous of Daddy's past.

"Forget the schedule, Jessica," says Daddy. "Go to the beach."

"Well, what do you think, Kate? The beach?"

I swirl my fork around in the spaghetti. Daddy and I used to play Frisbee at the beach. Once I got up to seventy-nine tosses without dropping it.

"Jessica just asked you a question, Katie."

"Oh, Michael, the beach will be fine," whispers Jessica.

"Of course it'll be fine," he says. "I wish *I* could go to the beach tomorrow."

I try to unswirl some of the spaghetti off my fork. If he wants me out here so badly, why can't we be alone for a while? I think he just wants to get me away from Mom to give her a bad time because she's always giving him a bad time. It's like those Chinese box sets. You open a box and there's another inside and inside that there's another and on and on. She gives him a bad time because he gives her one and on and on.

"What's the matter, Katie? Don't you want to go to the beach?"

What's the matter? Everything, that's all. Just everything. I don't have a family — forget normal, any kind will do. And that's just for openers. Why can't I reach Riley? Why doesn't she call me if she knows I'm here?

"Didn't you have fun with — what's her name?"

"Natalie," says Jessica.

"Right. Natalie. Didn't you have fun with her today?"

"She's really — well, a very interesting girl," says Jessica, eating just the meatballs out of her spaghetti. "Didn't you find her interesting, Kate?"

I don't want to think about Natalie. I don't want to think about her running away to take care of her little brother Dwight, or those fish she loves so much and carts around in McDonald's cups.

"Why are you playing with that spaghetti? You haven't said a word tonight."

"She's not playing with it, Michael."

"Well, what *is* she doing with it then? She's not eating it."

"She'll eat it, won't you, Kate?"

I twist more and more spaghetti on my fork. Where's Riley? That's what I need to know. Why hasn't she called me yet?

Little muscles twitch in Daddy's jaw. "Katie, you mustn't get withdrawn like this. Your mother spoils you, and I won't stand for it. That's your biggest problem. Your mother."

I put my fork down and burst into tears.

6

Sometimes when I wake up in the middle of the night I forget where I am. Beverly Hills? East 48th Street?

Tonight I wake up to absolute quiet. No New York traffic, no sirens racing up Third Avenue. Just the padded, tiptoe silence of Beverly Hills, as if everything, even the street, is carpeted. And it smells like California. Dry and sweet and clean instead of the mechanical smell of air conditioning.

My room is bright with moonlight. What made me wake up? The moonlight? A noise?

I was dreaming about music. Christina was playing the flute. *Was* I dreaming? Christina wouldn't play her flute in the middle of the night.

Now there's the wind and the starchy dry rustle of trees. I feel strange. Not sick, but worried about something I'll remember as soon as I'm wider awake. I'd rather go back to sleep so I won't have to remember. I squeeze my eyes shut.

The scene at dinner.

Why did I have to burst into tears like that? Daddy called it "fatigue." Jessica said she always cries a lot when she has jet lag. Nobody realized the real reason. I'm going crazy. I've turned into a thirteen-year-old crazy person. Even crazier than Natalie Blanchard.

Daddy's picture smiles at me in the moonlight. A big Cat-Man smile. On it he's written: "To my darling daughter Kate." Am I really his darling daughter Kate? Or am I the Ping-Pong ball he can have bounced to the west coast whenever he wants to bug Mom?

Do I love Daddy? Love is a funny word when you really think about it. Slippery. People use it so much that it gets transparent and light and slips away when you try to nail it down. I love Daddy the way he used to be. When the three of us were a family. And I still love him, but it's different now. It's like there's a wall between us and I don't know how to climb over it and he doesn't even know it's there.

Things are different now with Mom, too. We used to be really close. Before the divorce she'd do stuff that no other mother would do, like dress up as a ghost on Halloween and pretend she was a very tall little kid and go trick or treating with me. ("My goodness!" said one lady, handing Mom a Milky Way. "Are you in fifth or sixth grade? You're so tall!" "Sixth grade," squeaked Mom. And then we ran down the street laughing so hard we almost dropped our candy.) And one very hot July we pitched a tent in the backyard and camped out together for two days. Daddy wasn't too thrilled about that, but we had a wonderful time, reading books out loud to each other and eating peanut-butter-and-grape-jam sandwiches on Wonder bread, and at night we'd read with a flashlight.

What can happen between people in just two years is incredible. At first Mom kept busy all the time because she was so depressed about the divorce. She's worked as an interior decorator for as long as I can remember, but before she and Daddy started fighting all the time and got divorced, she always made sure she had a lot of time for me. After the divorce all she did was work, and then after a while it just got to be a habit, I guess. Last Christmas I wanted her to go shopping with me for presents for Riley and Daddy and everybody, but she never had time. So I had my friend Danielle call her at her office and pretend that she had an apartment that needed to be completely redone and could she please make an appointment. I listened on the extension.

"A client just canceled an appointment tomorrow morning," said Mom. "How about ten at my office?"

"Oh, ten would be splendid," said Danielle. "Perfect. Just perfect."

"And how many rooms in your apartment?"

"Eighteen."

I personally felt that Danielle was overdoing things, but Mom fell for it.

"Eighteen? Well! I'm looking forward to seeing you at ten tomorrow."

Then I showed up the next morning at ten and told her it was a joke ("Ha, ha, ha! I was listening the whole time on the extension, Mom!"), and since she didn't have an appointment, could we please go shopping together.

It was awful. She didn't think it was funny, and got mad and wouldn't go with me. Two years ago she would have thought it was very funny and clever and would have understood that I only did it because I needed her. She doesn't understand that kind of thing anymore. She's always in a bad mood unless Chad's around.

Daddy says Mom enjoys being in a bad mood.

Riley says bad moods are just a bad habit.

Riley.

Is she all right? Maybe she's sick. But if she were sick, somebody would call Daddy. I've been here one whole day and two nights. None of this makes any sense.

I want morning to come fast. I try to make my toes relax, and then my feet, my ankles, my legs, but it doesn't work. I close my eyes and try to see black velvet. I'm still wide-awake. All I want to do is go back to sleep so morning will come. Maybe if I try counting backward from a hundred —

There's a noise outside. It sounds like someone coughing. But it's so fleeting, like seeing something out of the corner of my eye, maybe I've imagined it. I listen. Just the Santa Ana wind blowing through the trees. I get out of bed and tiptoe to the windows. The bluish white moonlight makes the garden and pool and lawn look different: magical, like a stage set.

But there *is* something out there, and it isn't make-believe or magic. Almost hidden by fruit trees, two people are standing at the edge of the lawn. One of them begins walking toward the house and the other stays behind, waiting in the trees.

My heart's pounding. I don't know what to do. Should I start yelling? Get Daddy up?

I creep back into bed and pull the sheet up over my head.

I'm imagining this. I dreamed those two figures out there. Nobody's in the garden. Nobody's sneaking toward the house. Who would be out there in the middle of the night? Nobody.

Burglars, that's who.

But there's an alarm system.

Maybe they're very smart, experienced burglars who know how to get into the house without the alarm going off.

Maybe this is just the final stages of going crazy.

Now there's a different noise. And it isn't my imagination and it isn't any Santa Ana wind. It's coming from the hallway. As if something out there is feeling its way along the wall. I pull the sheet off my head and listen.

A tiny click and my door opens slowly. Then clicks shut again. I'm paralyzed. It's too late to yell. Someone is standing in the dim light by the doorway. I can hear them breathing. "Who is it?"

"Shh!" says a voice.

I peer into the shadows.

The figure moves across my room toward the windows and into the moonlight. "For heaven's sake, don't talk."

Riley. Wearing baggy slacks, a scarf tied around her head, dark glasses, and sneakers. She leans out of the window and waves a large white hankerchief. And then I hear one sweet flute note. "Everything's clear," she whispers. "Now, hurry up!"

"Hurry up?" I'm so surprised and excited to see her I can't even say so.

"Yes. *Hurry.*"

"Why?" I throw the sheet off and climb out of bed.

"Because I'm kidnapping you," says Riley.

7

W e're out of the house and creeping across the
lawn, staying in the shadows close to the
hedge.

"Why?" I whisper.

"Shh." Riley holds my hand tightly and pulls me
along. "Later."

I'm only wearing my pajamas, no robe or slippers.
The grass is dry and warm under my bare feet. The
pool reflects the moon and the air smells of oranges
and jasmine.

A light suddenly goes on in the house, upstairs in
Daddy's room. Riley pulls me closer to the hedge,
where we crouch down and don't move. We don't
even breathe. Nothing moves. The curtains stay
closed. Don't check my room. Don't investigate!

The light goes out. We wait another second, then
Riley squeezes my hand, and we continue to the end

of the garden and the gate that opens out to an alley that runs behind all the houses on this street. I feel like I'm in one of Daddy's shows. Maybe I'm about to turn into Cat-Woman. Maybe I'm dreaming all this.

There's Fritz waiting for us by the back gate. His round, friendly face glows in the moonlight; his beard makes him look like Santa Claus. "Oh, Fritz," I start to say, and Riley says, "Shh!" again. When we're in the alley, she takes a key from the pocket of her slacks, shuts the gate, and locks it. The key glitters and looks brand-new.

Sitting inside Riley's van, his nose pressed against the window, is the world's biggest, drooliest, friendliest dog — Wagner. Wagner's a Newfoundland and looks like a medium-size bear. The most dangerous thing he could do is drown you when he kisses you.

Every noise sounds loud — our footsteps crunching on the unpaved alley, the door of the van opening with a loud click and closing with an even louder click, Wagner panting. When I put my arms around his big neck, he washes my face with his huge tongue. Fritz is at the wheel and I squeeze into the passenger seat with Riley. Balloons bob around in the back of the van.

Fritz starts the engine and then, without any lights on (which we don't need anyway, the moon is so bright), he drives very slowly away. Tall hedges and high walls line the alley. Nobody says anything. Wagner pants. One of the balloons bobs into the front seat and Riley pushes it away. Out on the main road Fritz turns on the headlights and drives faster.

Riley starts to chuckle. "Well!"

"You did it!" says Fritz.

"*We* did it!" She puts her arms around me and holds me close for a minute. She smells of Ivory soap. "Oh, how I've missed you, Katie!" She pulls the scarf off her head, takes off her glasses, and tries to fasten her hair with little combs. Her hair is unruly and thick like Daddy's, but a silvery, shimmery color, not dark like his. "Let me look at you." We grin at each other. "You look *wonderful!* A little sleepy, but beautiful."

Dark houses, long gardens, walls, and trees speed past us; everything dreaming and sleeping in the moonlight. I give Riley's hand a squeeze and she squeezes mine back. "This is really happening, isn't it?"

"Of course it's really happening."

"You're kidnapping me."

"Yes!"

"They won't know it's you. I mean, they're going to think I've *really* been kidnapped!"

"Nonsense. They're going to know exactly who did it."

"They are?"

"Yes. Your father is going to think your mother did it, and your mother is going to think your father did it."

"You *want* them to think that?"

"Of course!"

"*Why?*"

"What do your parents have to do to make you happy? They have to get together and talk about what's best for you. They can't ship you back and forth across the country like an airmail package whenever they want to show each other who's in charge. This is simply a method of getting them together to talk."

"You don't think it's a little drastic?"

"Do you?"

"No!" And I hug her hard.

"Wasn't anything else to do," says Fritz. Ahead of us looms the big San Diego Freeway sign, and he gets into the southbound lane.

"When your mother hears you're missing," says Riley, "she's going to think it's a plot of your father's to get back at her for the time she took you to Bermuda instead of sending you here for spring vacation. And he's going to think your mother planned this because he threatened to have her arrested. And your mother, with her formidable temper, will be on a plane to California within twenty-four hours."

"Not just send her lawyer?"

"Oh, not for this, Katie. This is kidnapping. This time he'll have gone too far, and she'll want you back, and the only way to get you back will be to come here in person and find you herself. They'll be forced to confront one another."

"Don't you think that could be dangerous?"

"No, I think it'll be healthy. A good fight never hurt anybody."

"And then what happens?" I ask, as if Riley's telling me a story.

"And then, since they're both intelligent adults, they'll figure out what I've done, and I expect the two of them to show up in San Pedro within forty-eight hours. *Together*. And ready to talk about *you*."

"Holy cow."

53

"A humdinger of a plan, isn't it?" asks Fritz.

"It sure is." Only Riley would dream up something this fantastic, this exciting. This *sensible*.

"Wasn't that Christina something!" Fritz chuckles. "She managed the key business and those flute signals like she's been doing this sort of thing all her life."

"She had a copy of the gate key made for us," explains Riley. "And then she hid it for us to pick up outside in the alley."

"She seemed so happy tonight. I couldn't figure out what was going on. And I was so worried when you didn't call me back and when nobody answered the phone at six-fifteen in the morning, and then when Hank pretended he couldn't hear me —"

"Oh, wasn't Hank *wonderful*," says Riley.

"He could be an actor," says Fritz.

"Katie, I was afraid if I talked to you on the phone I'd give the whole plan away. And I wanted so much for it to work!"

I put my head on her shoulder. "It's going to work," I say. The windows are open and the warm night air blows against our faces. Wagner nuzzles the back of my neck. This is the best plan Riley has ever come up with.

Another balloon bobs into the front and Fritz catches it before it goes out the window. "A party, day after tomorrow."

"Tomorrow, actually." Riley peers at the dashboard clock. "It's almost four."

We switch from the San Diego Freeway to the Harbor Freeway. SAN PEDRO — SOUTH, says the sign. I know this route by heart. I've never been on it

54

at four o'clock in the morning, though; and I've never seen a freeway this empty. The moon hangs low in the sky toward the ocean, so huge and bright we can see the craters on it. The summery air is clean because there are so few cars. The van hums down the freeway.

When I open my eyes we're at the end of the freeway. San Pedro. Clusters of light are scattered over the harbor. The streets are steep and twisty as roller coasters. This is where Riley has lived for forty years. In the same house. I love it that she's never moved. Maybe people keep better track of themselves when they stay in the same house for years and years.

Trees and red masses of bougainvillaea hide Riley's house from the road. We park in the driveway. Wagner is so excited he makes little yelping noises way back in his throat, as if he knows he'll be in trouble if he barks out loud at this hour.

There's the bottom porch step that sags and that no one's ever figured out how to fix, and the creaky swing on the porch, and the pots of red geraniums, and the screen door that bangs louder than any other screen door in the world.

I can smell the ocean mixed with the dry, grassy wind. The ocean is only two blocks away, and you can see it from the bedroom windows upstairs. The sky has the blurry, smudged look it gets just before dawn. As we walk up to the front porch, something warm and furry circles around my bare ankles. I reach down and pick up a cat, trying to tell in the shadowy dark which one it is. "Yeager?" I whisper.

55

"Koufax," Riley whispers back. She names all her cats after Dodgers.

I carry Koufax into the house. Fritz catches the screen door so it won't bang. The house is quiet and still, everyone upstairs sleeping.

At the top of the stairs the room I've slept in every summer is waiting — a lamp turned on, the curtains moving in the wind, white sheets turned down. I love this room. It's always been here waiting for me. The same brass bed, the dresser with the glass knobs, the rocking chair that belonged to my great-grandmother. On the bare wood floor is the rug that Riley braided out of old clothes one winter. It's a room you can walk into with sandy feet right after the beach and not hurt anything. Riley's whole house is like that.

I crawl into bed and Riley pulls the sheet up over my shoulders. She kisses me. I fall right to sleep.

8

"**Y**ou want to play crazy eights?"

Hank's voice. Right in my ear.

I keep my eyes shut.

"First she's got to have breakfast."

Riley's voice.

I didn't dream last night. I did not go crazy. I'm really in Riley's house in San Pedro, kidnapped from Beverly Hills. I keep my eyes closed. I love lying here just thinking about it; it's like a present I'm holding in my hand, all wrapped up and waiting to be opened. Something very soft pats my face, then crawls under the sheet, purring. I peek. Orange fur. Yeager.

"She's got an eye open," says Hank.

I open both eyes and look into Hank's brown ones behind his wire-rimmed glasses. His chin rests on the edge of the bed about eight inches away. I can smell strawberry jam. He looks like he's wearing a pink mustache. His wheat-color hair stands up in sharp little cowlicks.

"Hi, Hank."

"Hi, Kate."

"How are you?"

"Okay."

"Did you miss me?"

"Yeah. You want to play crazy eights now?"

"She wants to have pancakes and bacon first, don't you, Katie?" says Riley. "You run and tell Fritz she'll be down for breakfast in ten minutes."

The bacon and coffee smell like the summers when I was little and stayed here for all of July and August.

"And take Yeager with you." Riley grabs Yeager from under the covers and hands him to Hank. "He needs his breakfast, too." Yeager ducks his head into Hank's neck and purrs. Hank kisses the top of his head as he carries him out.

"Well, my darling Katie!" Riley perches at the foot of my bed. "How do you feel?"

"I feel wonderful."

"So do I." She's got on her gardening clothes — blue jeans, a blue work shirt, and sneakers — and her hair has gotten lose from the combs again, spilling around her face.

"What do you think Daddy's doing?"

She checks her watch. "He has called the police."

"How do you think he feels?"

"Mad."

"You're sure that's good?"

"Positive. It's the only way to get them together."
She squeezes my toes through the sheets. "Being polite and doing the right thing doesn't always work, you know. Sometimes you really have to do something terrible to get people's attention."

"I'm glad I'm here."

"So am I! How have you been? Your letters have been scarce as hen's teeth this summer."

"I've been okay, I guess, but the summer's been awful. Camp was lousy and New York is too hot. I've been working on this plan to find Mom a terrific boyfriend who would make a good stepfather —"

"How on earth do you go about that?"

"It's not easy. I've been inviting men I like to go to the park with us on weekends, things like that. I'm very casual about it. But Mom went out and found herself a boyfriend. A real dip named Chad. I'm also trying to find somebody for Daddy, but that's harder."

Riley always listens like she's memorizing every word, as if she's holding her breath while I talk. "Well," she says, "the summer's about to improve."

"It already has."

"Now, I've got to find you something to wear." She opens a drawer and pulls out a pair of shorts and a T-shirt. "You left these your last visit. They ought to still fit."

"Haven't you noticed? I've grown about a foot since then. That's what Daddy says."

"He does, does he? Has he also mentioned what a raving beauty you're turning into? Probably not; it makes fathers very nervous."

"Oh, Riley —"

"But don't let it go to your head. Here —" She tosses me the clothes. "There's some underwear in the top drawer and I put a new toothbrush in your bathroom. Rise and shine! It's almost nine o'clock."

Nine o'clock in Riley's house is like noon anywhere else.

Fritz is concentrating on flipping pancakes. He sees me and frowns. This is not the friendly Santa Claus face of last night. Nobody can fool around when Fritz is at work in his kitchen.

"You're late," he says to me.

"Well, I had a busy night."

He's not amused. "Sit down, sit down! Everything will get cold!"

"Well, that might be a blessing this morning," says Myra, who's sitting at the kitchen table making party favors out of clothespins. "Dearest Katie," she says and kisses my cheek. "How wonderful to have you here."

"Thank you," I say. "It's good to be here. That's a beautiful dress, Myra."

Myra's very vain about clothes and is always dressed up. She likes pinks and oranges and purples, so it's hard not to notice her clothes. She's very tiny and the bright colors make her look like a tropical bird.

"It's too hot for hot food and hot plates," she says.

"Button your lip, Myra," says Fritz. If Myra ever has a second nervous breakdown, Fritz will be the cause of it. He pours melted butter over a stack of golden, perfect pancakes, puts two slices of bacon on the plate, and sets it down in front of me.

I can never understand how someone as solid and barrellike as Fritz can produce such delicate, airy pancakes.

Fritz takes cooking seriously, which is a good thing because no one else in Riley's house does. He doesn't just cook ordinary food either; he cooks what he calls gourmet meals. Fancy food. Once he made something called escargots, which is actually snails and really gross, and Yeager and Koufax got up on the counter and tried to get the snails out of the shells with their claws. Fritz got so mad we had to hide the cats, because he said he was going to murder them and nobody knew for sure if he was exaggerating.

"Hot syrup's coming," he announces.

"I'm *starving*, Fritz!" I never did get any of that spaghetti off my fork last night. Last night seems like a million years ago.

"More cakes for me, please," says Hank, coming in from the garden. Through the open door I see Riley back at work, Wagner following her around the garden.

"*More* pancakes?" says Fritz. "You've had about a dozen. You're going to explode."

"Not Hank," says Hank.

"What do you think of barley earrings?" Myra asks. "I was going to use Cheerios, but they're too big."

"What's barley?" asks Hank.

"Grain. One normally puts it in soup." She's making ballerinas out of the clothespins, and dozens of little cotton-puff wigs are spread out in front of her.

"Barley earrings sound terrific." Everything sounds terrific to me this morning.

"Here we go." Fritz hands Hank a plate.

Hank looks at it. "No pigs."

"It's bacon, not pigs," says Fritz.

Hank shakes his head very slowly. "Pigs."

Fritz takes the bacon off Hank's plate and then hands the plate back. "Hank has become a vegetarian," he says to me. "He's just figured out where meat comes from."

Hank sits down next to me. "You want to play crazy eights after breakfast?"

"Sure."

"It's too hot to do anything else," says Myra, carefully drawing the ballerina's eyes on with a tiny brush.

Hank peeks under his pancakes as if to see if any bacon is hiding under them, then asks me, "How does it feel to be kidnapped?"

"Pretty good," I answer.

Austin drifts into the kitchen like a tall, slender ghost. "Coffee," he says, and then notices me at the table. "Kate!"

"Hi, Austin."

"You're kidnapped."

"Yes."

He nods and smiles. When Austin comes down from his studio and actually says a complete sentence, everybody treats it like a message from a foreign country. They puzzle over it for days, as if it needs to be translated.

He pours himself a cup of coffee from the pot on the stove, says "Kate" again, and wanders out of the kitchen. I can't figure out if Austin is very shy or if his thoughts are so complicated he simply can't share them with us. He has long dark hair, which Riley cuts for him in the backyard when somebody remarks that Austin's hair is down to his shoulders again. He's just not aware of these things. He simply forgets to have his hair cut. He's also very thin because he's always forgetting to eat. All he cares about is working in his attic studio.

I suddenly wonder: Has Mom ever met Austin? He's a little young for her but he'd certainly make an interesting stepfather.

"I considered putting false eyelashes on them but realized that would create untold difficulties," says Myra, holding up one of the ballerinas.

"Good pancakes, Fritz." I scoop up the last bite and try to imagine Mom getting serious about Austin. It isn't easy.

"It's no picnic, cooking in this kitchen," complains Fritz, as he has ever since I can remember. Yeager jumps up on the counter and meows at him. *"Down!"* Fritz shouts. "See that? Nothing like that would ever happen at sea. No discipline around here. Cats do anything they please."

Yeager jumps up on top of the refrigerator and hides behind the ivy plant and books up there. Everything in the kitchen shines in the morning sun: the copper pots that Fritz keeps polished over the stove, the green plants curling down from baskets over the sink, the round wooden table that Daddy sat at when he was my age. On one corner of the table there are two M's, Daddy's initials. Riley told me he carved them into the table with a penknife he got for his eighth birthday.

The phone rings; sudden and unexpected.

We all look at it hanging on the wall by the door as if a loud, rude stranger has suddenly burst into the kitchen. Then we look at each other. It rings again. Nobody moves.

"Do you think it's" — And everybody nods before I can finish saying — "my father."

"We could let the answering machine answer," whispers Myra.

"Oh, good grief," says Fritz. He wipes his hands on a towel, clears his throat, and picks up the receiver. "Hello? Yes, yes, of course. I'll get her right away." Without looking at any of us, he walks to the back door and calls to Riley in the garden. "Telephone for you, Riley. Your son."

Her son. My father. Daddy. On the other end of that line. Practically in the room with us. I want to tell him not to worry. I want to tell him to worry a lot. I feel like I'm going to start giggling. I'm not cut out for a life of suspense.

Riley takes off her straw hat and gardening gloves, sets a basket of strawberries on the counter, fastens her hair, and picks up the phone. She looks like an actor about to begin a scene. "Hello, Michael, how lovely to hear from you. . . . Diana has done *what*? Are you sure?"

My hand is over my mouth. I always giggle in tense situations. It makes Mom crazy. "Wipe that smile off your face!" she'll yell when we're having a fight, and that makes me so hysterical I think I'll never stop giggling.

"The *police*, Michael?" asks Riley.

Fritz stands motionless by the stove. Myra and Hank sit with me, both resting their elbows on the table, chins cupped in their hands, watching Riley as if they're watching television.

"But Diana's in New York. How could she have kidnapped Kate? . . . How could she have been on Kate's plane? You would have seen her at the airport. . . . You didn't? Who did? . . . Your agent! Oh, Michael, I know you're a busy man, but you made such a *fuss* about getting Kate back to Los Angeles for a week, surely you could have met her plane, dear. She's still a little girl."

My thumb hurts, I've bitten the nail down so far.

"Well, I'm fine. Don't worry about me, worry about Kate. . . . Michael, don't yell. My ear hurts when you yell. . . . Don't be silly, Diana's not that bad. . . . Yes, let me know the minute you hear something. . . . Love to you, too. Good-bye!" She puts the receiver back on the hook. "Well! Right on the button!"

"What did he say?" we all ask at once.

"Exactly what I said he would. He's absolutely furious. He thinks that Diana might have been on Kate's plane in disguise — he's so angry he's become irrational. Or that she followed on another plane or had an accomplice."

"What's a complice?" asks Hank.

"Partner in crime. You are my accomplice, and so are Fritz and Myra and Christina, because we all worked together to kidnap Kate." Yeager jumps down from the refrigerator and onto Riley's lap. She scratches him behind the ears and he starts to purr. "Oh, what a jerk he is sometimes!"

"Yeager?" Hank looks shocked.

"No, no, not Yeager. Kate's daddy. He was such a nice little boy. He collected coins. He worried about animals; always bringing home stray cats and dogs. He once catalogued all his books. What went wrong?"

"Oh, Riley, you did a great job." I eat one of the strawberries she just picked. "He's just gone downhill recently."

"Don't upset yourself, Riley." Fritz pours her a cup of tea. "He's still a nice fellow."

"Frankly, I find him quite charming," says Myra.

"Oh, *charm*," says Riley. "Horsefeathers! What good is charm? What about his *character*? His problem is that he's all charm and no substance." She looks at me, really looks at me. Her eyes are as blue as the flowers on her china cup, and her face is all lines and bones, as if the stuff that isn't important has just melted away. "The best thing about being a grandparent is that it's a second chance. And this time around I don't have to worry about all the trivia, like shoes fitting properly, and grades, and straight teeth. This time I can concentrate on the essentials."

"Essentials?" I repeat.

"Character." She sips her tea, smiling. "Backbone."

"Doesn't Kate have a backbone?" asks Hank.

"Yes, but not enough of one."

"What do you mean?" I feel insulted. "I've got tons of backbone!"

"Riley, she's just a little girl." Myra pats my arm.

"I'm thirteen. I'm a teenager!"

"None of us ever have enough backbone and character," says Riley. "It's something we must always work at. Like good posture or extending our vocabularies."

Character and backbone remind me of spinach. Good for you, but not something you'd go out and look for.

Yeager jumps off her lap and onto the floor. "Now, that fellow has both." Riley points to Yeager. "Character *and* good posture."

"He's got a lousy vocabulary, though," I say.

"What he's got is fleas," says Fritz. "Fleas all over this house. You never find fleas on a ship."

"I keep telling you, Fritz, this is not a ship." Riley finishes her tea and puts the cup in the sink. "This is a house, and if you have pets in your house, you have fleas."

"The Randolphs never had fleas." Myra sighs. The Randolphs also never had dirt, cloudy weather, or colds.

"Did they have any cats or dogs?" Hank asks.

"Well, no."

"That's why they didn't have fleas." Hank shuffles

the deck of cards that he keeps in the pocket of his shorts.

Fritz puts the dishes in the dishwasher. "Everybody get out of here. I'm going to start on the cake for tomorrow. I'm trying a new recipe."

"The party!" says Riley. "I'd forgotten all about it. What time do we have to be there? Where's the party book? Don't we have two in a row?"

Fritz takes a three-ring loose-leaf notebook down from the top of the refrigerator, blows cat hairs off it, and hands it to Riley. She leafs through it to the right page and then reads, "Four o'clock. Nine guests, all girls, and the theme is 'come as what you want to be when you're grown up.' That ought to be interesting. Holly Haskell's tenth birthday. They live in Palos Verdes so we ought to allow thirty minutes to get there. And then we have one in Redondo Beach the next day."

"Is Kate coming?" asks Hank.

"Of course Kate is coming," Riley says instantly. And then her forehead knits together. "But how? They might recognize Cat-Man's daughter."

Everybody stares at me. Myra makes a little clicking noise with her tongue, like a clock ticking. Fritz is frowning so hard it looks like his eyes will disappear. "She'll have to be disguised," he says.

"And shoes," says Riley. "What on earth will we do about shoes for you?"

"She's got to be disguised but not wear any shoes." Myra looks up at the ceiling. "Hmm."

"We need a clown," says Hank.

"A clown?" Myra and Fritz say it at the same time.

"A clown." A big smile lights up Riley's face. "A *clown*. What a marvelous idea, Hank. A clown's face would be a perfect disguise and you would wear shoes that were too big for you. And you'd be able to help us."

A clown. All I can think of is Ronald McDonald. "But what would I do?"

"You can help Hank pick up garbage," says Hank.

"Garbage?"

"Birthday present wrappings and ribbon," explains Riley. "Not actual garbage."

"You forget the party where the guests threw carrot sticks and hamburgers at each other," says Fritz.

"That doesn't happen often, though," Riley points out. "And you could help Austin by posing with the kids for pictures."

"And you can help me set up the puppet stage," says Fritz.

"And help me set up the table," says Myra.

"I need help with balloons," says Hank.

"Good heavens, Katie," says Riley. "How did we ever manage without you?"

9

What's happening in Beverly Hills? What's happening on East 48th Street? I feel like Riley has set up World War III. We should be hearing the bombs any minute. But so far it's quiet and still, and too hot to go outside. Once in a while there's a gust of wind and the trees and grass bend, changing position with a scratchy sound. Upstairs Riley is rehearsing for the puppet show for tomorrow's party. Myra watches soap operas in the den. (*"Roger, I don't think I can take anymore,"* a woman called Melinda says, her voice blaring out into the quiet as if she and Roger are sitting right there in the den with Myra, shouting at each other.) Fritz is in the kitchen playing his banjo. Hank and I get orange Popsicles out of the freezer.

"Now crazy eights?" he asks.

"Okay." We go out into the front hallway and sit

on the floor by the foot of the stairs. When there's a gust of wind, we can feel a slight draft here through the screen door. The cats found this place first. It you want to know where the coolest spot is on a hot day, just find out where the cats are sleeping. Also the warmest spot on a cold day. Koufax stretches out under the telephone table, his white stomach showing, and Yeager lies on top of the table, all four paws and his tail hanging over the edge. Wagner sleeps by the door, making a faint snoring sound.

Hank slurps at his Popsicle and tries to shuffle the cards with one hand.

The rug that runs down the front hallway is old and flat and faded, smooth under our bare legs. I know this rug so well I've never even noticed the pattern until now.

Hank starts to deal the cards.

Sometimes I think Riley's house is filled with ghosts. Not ghosts of dead people but ghosts of us.

Every Friday night during summers when I was little: Daddy on the front porch yelling, "Riley, where's Katykins?" And the screen door would bang and there they'd be, standing in this hallway — nice, normal parents who loved each other.

Ghosts. That was a long time ago.

"Kate?" says Hank. "You look funny. Are you going to cry?"

"No." I pick up the eight cards he's dealt me and arrange them by suit. Four clubs, two spades, one diamond, and an eight of hearts. He takes the top card off the deck, three of spades, and I put my nine of spades on it.

"Oh." Hank takes off his glasses and rubs his

71

eyes, then scratches his ankle. "Oh." He doesn't have any nines or spades, so he draws cards from the deck until he gets the ten of spades.

I run my finger over the design in the rug. There are diamonds inside of diamonds and along the edge a design of flowers and trees. Triangle trees like Christmas trees.

Christmas ghosts. We always spent Christmas here before the divorce. Fritz and Daddy put up the tree and Riley unpacked the ornaments one by one, always remembering where each one came from, who gave it to her, or who made it. The piny smell of the tree and logs burning in the fireplace, and cinnamon and candles. "Two strands of tinsel at the very most, Katie," Mom said whenever I got lazy and put huge globs of tinsel on the tree. Fritz's sugar cookies decorated with green and red icing and tiny silver balls, and Myra's wreath for the front door made out of walnuts and acorns and pods off the trees. The year Daddy got a good part on TV, his first big part, he went out and bought us all too many presents. Mom, who's not the kind of person who squeals, squealed every time she opened one of her presents, and each time she'd jump up and kiss Daddy.

Now it's alternating Christmases and either Mom isn't here or Daddy and Riley aren't there, and it's not the same anymore. The last Christmas I spent here Daddy brought a girlfriend who had purple fingernails about six inches long and kept telling us that someday she was going to have a tree sprayed silver with all silver ornaments, so everything would match. Definitely not in the running for future terrific stepmother.

72

"Kate, it's your turn," says Hank.

I put an eight of hearts on his card.

"What is it?" he asks.

"Eight of hearts."

"It doesn't have to be hearts. That's why it's called crazy eights. You can make your eights whatever you want."

I look at my cards. "Okay. Clubs."

"Clubs," he mutters, frowning at his cards.

When I was really little the tree would be a surprise on Christmas morning. The doors to the living room would be kept shut until after the tree was decorated and all the presents were under it. Christmas morning Riley would open the doors and there would be the tree, all lit and shining, standing right in the middle of the room with the presents heaped beneath it, and everybody would clap and Riley would say, "Oh, my! Look what Santa Claus brought us!"

Except for the Christmas I was six. That year our cat Robinson got locked up overnight with the tree by mistake and Robinson ate all the tinsel from the lower branches, knocked off balls and smashed them around on the floor, and unwrapped some of the presents. That Christmas morning no one clapped and Riley did not say, "Oh, my, look what Santa Claus brought us." She said, "I've had it! I'll give that cat away. I don't care if it is Christmas, I'm going to get rid of him." Which she didn't, of course, but she was awfully mad at Robinson for a while.

"Why don't you like to play crazy eights?" asks Hank.

"I love to play it."

"But you're not paying any attention."

"I'm sorry. I was just remembering things."

"What kind of things?"

I chew on my Popsicle stick. "Christmases here when I was little. What it used to be like."

"What was it like?"

"Different."

"How?"

"I guess not really different. The only thing that was different was that my parents were together so I was different. Does that make sense?"

Hank thinks for a minute, then shakes his head. "No."

"It doesn't?"

"Not to me."

"Oh, well. Let's finish the game."

In the kitchen Fritz is thrumming away on his banjo and in the den we hear Roger saying to Melinda: *"Give me a chance. We can work this out. We can work this out, Melinda!"*

"We can work this out, Kate!" cries Hank.

"Very funny." I squint at my cards trying to figure out what to do next.

Upstairs Riley is still rehearsing. "Oh, what big ears you have!" she cries in a sharp, high voice. Then her voice suddenly changes. "Oh, good heavens —" and she's out of her room, clattering down the stairs. "Kate, upstairs, upstairs! Stay calm, everybody —"

I scramble to my feet. "What is it?"

"Police!" she says in a loud whisper.

"Police?" What would police be doing at Riley's

house? And then I remember. World War III. I'm suddenly so scared I can't even breathe.

"They pulled up out in front, right there at the end of the driveway." She peeks out the screen door, standing to the side so she can't be seen.

The door to the den opens. *"Roger, I've got to do something for myself. I've got to discover who I am."* Myra comes out into the hallway. "What's going on?" she asks. Back in the den Roger asks, *"Melinda, I love you, doesn't that mean anything?"*

"Turn down the TV a bit, Myra. Do you mind? The police are outside."

"Police?!"

"Try to understand, Roger," says Melinda.

"Myra, I can't think with that show blaring in there."

Myra runs back into the den and clicks off the set.

"It looks like there's just one out there," says Riley, still peeking out the door. "Hank, you take Kate upstairs. Don't let her out of your sight."

My heart is pounding so loud and fast I'm surprised the police can't hear it.

"I'll complice," says Hank.

"What?"

"I'll be your complice."

"*Ac*complice, Hank. Right. Now hurry upstairs, both of you. Myra, go tell Fritz that a policeman is coming to visit, and you'd better run up and tell Austin, too. Everybody just stay calm and let me handle this fellow." She tries to capture her hair in the little combs on top of her head, but her hair just keeps looking wilder. "There's nothing to worry about!"

Hank puts his soft, sticky hand in mine and we hurry upstairs to my room. There we sit in the closet. The policeman probably won't search the house, but it makes me feel better just in case.

"Stay right here," whispers Hank.

"Don't worry. I will. You, too."

We both sound like we're having trouble breathing.

"I'm scared."

"It's okay, Hank. He's just going to talk to Riley. Probably ask her a lot of questions about me." What if he *does* search the house?

Winter clothes brush the tops of our heads. Shopping bags filled with gift wrapping and ribbon hang from the hooks, the ribbons curling down and trailing against our faces. The closet smells of mothballs and wood.

"It's too hot in here," says Hank.

I open the door and we blink in the sudden light.

"I'm hungry." He points to his stomach. "It's growling."

"The policeman will be gone soon."

"How do you know?"

"Well, he can't stay here all day, can he?"

"Why not?"

"He just can't, that's all. He's a policeman. He can't just hang around all day and talk. He's here on business and that won't take long."

Will it?

We wait.

"We're going to starve up here," says Hank finally.

A hot breeze blows my curtains out like little white sails.

"We should have brought some cards with us." Hank's glasses are beginning to slide down his nose.

Why is that policeman taking so long? Maybe he's down there — what's the word? drilling? — grilling Riley. Doesn't he think my mother kidnapped me?

"Hank, I'm going to sneak out into the hall and listen to what's going on. You stay here. I'll be right back."

"I'm not supposed to let you out of my sight."

"It's okay. They won't see me. I can just listen to them from the top of the stairs."

There's an oak hatrack near the top of the stairs, with raincoats and sweaters that I can hide behind if I can get to it. But if the policeman decides to leave and goes to the front door as I'm crossing the upstairs hall, he'll see me. I listen. A murmur of voices from the living room. I cross the hall quickly and crouch down behind the coats. Their voices still aren't distinct. I've got to get closer to the living room.

The only way is to pile some coats over my head and creep down the stairs. If he starts to come out of the living room I can just curl up on the stairs and pretend I'm a pile of raincoats.

Halfway down the stairs I hear the policeman say, "Tommy's the greatest."

I stay where I am and try to breathe more quietly.

"Time will tell," says Riley.

"There's nobody like Tommy."

Tommy? Who's Tommy?

77

"He's got Steve," the policeman goes on. "Steve's just like a rock out there. And Davey —"

Steve? Davey? Tommy?

"Frankly, I'd like to see more of Yeager," says Riley. "More iced tea?"

Yeager. The Dodgers. Riley's got him talking about baseball!

I tiptoe back up the stairs, dump the raincoats, and tell Hank, who's still in the closet.

"Riley loves baseball," he says.

"She used to take me to a game almost every week."

"She takes me to a lot of games. Once I ate fourteen hot dogs."

"No, you didn't, Hank. Don't tell fibs."

"Five. Five hot dogs?"

I shake my head.

"Two?"

"Two. I believe you ate two."

"But I could've eaten fourteen. Just nobody would buy me fourteen."

I'm starting to get hungry, too. "You know what I'd like right now?"

"What?"

"A burrito with extra sauce from Taco Bell."

"That sounds pretty good."

Koufax slinks around the door, orange and glowing in my sunny room. He makes a puzzled meow when he sees us sitting on the closet floor and then butts his head against our knees and purrs.

"I don't eat hot dogs anymore," says Hank. "I don't eat animals."

"I wish you'd stop talking about eating." I scratch Koufax behind his ears. I'm going to have about six cats when I grow up. Mom's allergic to cats so we can't get any. Daddy said she wasn't allergic to them until he started playing Cat-Man.

A car starts outside, and we jump up and look out the window. The police car is backing out of the driveway.

"Lunch!" says Hank.

10

Riley's waiting for us at the foot of the stairs. "Nice fellow, but he didn't know beans about baseball. Come finish the iced tea with me."

Hank and I follow her into the living room. "Does he suspect anything? Why did he come here?"

"He doesn't suspect a thing. He said the police believe your father's theory of your mother kidnapping you, but they can't take that sort of thing for granted. He wanted to know if I'd heard from you or thought you might have run away. I told him you hadn't called me and that you didn't seem to be the type to run away."

"Did he believe you?"

"Of course he believed me. *I* believed me. I was telling the truth. You have not tried to reach me by telephone since you disappeared from your father's house, and you are not the kind of person to run away." She hands us each a glass of iced tea with mint floating on the top. "As a matter of fact, he called me a very strong and brave woman. Hank, I believe I'd hold on to that glass with both hands if I were you. And Katie, he said your mother is coming to Los Angeles."

"When?"

"Tomorrow."

"Oh, Riley, just like you said! Everything is working out exactly the way you planned."

"I'm hungry," says Hank.

"Ask Fritz to fix you something," says Riley. "Or fix it yourself. And here, take the pitcher with you and your glass. Hold on tight."

"I can't reach the peanut butter."

"Fritz will get it down for you. Come on, Katie, it's too nice a day to stay inside. Let's go work in the garden."

"I'm never going to make any kid of mine weed." I pull a big prickly weed out of a hill of zucchini vines.

"Well, if you don't, you'll have to do it all yourself." Riley pours a can of Schlitz into five small dishes for snail bait. Snails are crazy for beer and jump right into it and drown, so she doesn't have to use snail poison, which also kills the birds.

Wagner sticks his nose into one of the dishes and gulps down some beer. "Oh, Wagner!" cries Riley. "No beer!"

Wagner ducks his chin until he catches his chain collar in his mouth and then begins to prance in a circle, his tail up, his neck arched just like a circus pony. He does this dance with his collar whenever he gets excited.

"And what a silly dog you are!"

Round and round goes Wagner until finally he drops his chain with a snort and sits down.

"Couldn't you train him to help you weed?" I ask.

"Never. He much prefers to dance."

"So do I."

"Toss me those weeds and I'll chop them up for the compost pile." Riley's gardening shears flash in the sun as she chops up the weeds like she's making a salad.

A compost pile is made out of all the weeds and garbage from the kitchen and all the stuff that isn't plastic, glass, or metal. You layer it with dirt, you wet it down, and pretty soon it all turns sweet smelling and rich and you can grow anything in it.

I sit back on my heels and wipe my forehead. "Remember when I helped you make the compost pile one summer and you told me that's what life is like? One big compost pile. I didn't know what you meant then."

Her shears snap at the weeds. "And now?"

"And now I know! At least I know about the garbage in life, like my parents fighting about me all the time, and all these trips I take back and forth —"

She stops chopping weeds and looks at me.

"You said garbage can make things grow. Real garbage and the bad stuff in life."

Riley nods.

"Well, what am I going to get out of all this garbage I'm going through?"

82

She grins at me. "Character and backbone!"

"Oh, terrific."

She spreads the chopped weeds over the top of the compost pile, then empties a bag of coffee grounds, eggshells, and orange peel over that and waters it all.

"Have you ever had a compost pile go bad? Just turn to worse garbage and smell?"

"Never!"

Hank comes out to watch us. He crosses his arms in front of his chest. His shorts are too big and droop down to his knees.

"Idle hands are the devil's tools," says Riley.

"What does that mean?" he asks.

"That means you better come over here and start to weed!"

"Between the spokes, Fritz! Not on them."

"*On* them. You're going to send me to an early grave, Myra!"

In the kitchen Myra and Fritz argue how the dishes should go into the dishwasher.

"And the plates should face the center."

"*This* is the way it's done."

Riley and I sit on the porch swing in the dark. The sound of bathwater running comes from the open window above us, and there's the low hum of Austin's voice as he reads a story to Hank. The air is so sweet with flowers and ocean smells and memories of past summers, it almost hurts to breathe it in. Everything whispers and rustles.

Riley keeps the swing moving, pushing with her foot when it slows down. Light spills from the living-

83

room window. She stares up at the porch ceiling where it's cracked and flaky with paint.

"We really ought to sand that down and repaint it one of these days," she says.

Wagner sits next to the swing, alert to all the night sounds, sniffing the air. When Riley reaches over and strokes his head, his tail thumps on the porch floor.

"You know what I really want?" I say.

"What?" asks Riley.

"A family like my friend Shannon has."

"Why?"

"Because they're so normal. They all have so much fun and love each other. Sometimes I get worried that I'm not going to find these perfect stepparents that I'm looking for. And if I do, Mom and Daddy won't like them. And what if they just get even madder about your kidnapping me? It'll be the same old garbage again — 'Michael, you can have her for half of Valentine's Day if you don't get me upset.' 'Diana, I want her sent out for an hour on St. Patrick's day, or I'll have you arrested.' "

"You do a very good imitation of your parents," laughs Riley.

"That's how they really are."

"I know, but I think it's just a phase."

"That's what Mom keeps telling me I'm going through."

We can hear Hank laughing and splashing in his tub. A car drives down the street, its headlights blurred through the trees and hedges. Fritz and Myra have stopped arguing; the dishwasher whirs in the kitchen.

"Did they want me?" I ask.

"Yes, very much."

"Did they love each other?"

"What do you think?"

"Well, I thought they did. But people who love each other don't get divorced."

"They once loved each other very, very much. That's what you must know and remember. When they had you, they loved each other."

"Maybe if they hadn't loved each other so much, they wouldn't hate each other so much now."

"That's true. Very true and wise."

I don't feel very wise. I reach for Riley's hand and hold it. She's got a Band-Aid on her thumb, and her hand is hard and full of tiny lines. "They used to fight about stupid things that didn't matter. Why did they have to go get a divorce?"

"I don't know, Katie." She shakes her head. "They got stubborn and hurt and angry and they hung on to everything that went wrong. Their lives changed so suddenly when your father got that part on television. It isn't easy to live with someone else day after day under any circumstances, but when there's suddenly so much money, and all those silly fans of his . . . People expect marriage to be easy, and when it isn't, sometimes they just give up. A bad memory is essential for happy relationships. Unfortunately, your parents both have excellent memories."

"Is that what happened to you and Grandfather? You just gave up?"

"Well, in a way." She stops pushing the swing with her foot and is very still. "But that was a much more complicated situation."

"How?"

"Your grandfather fell in love with someone else. Actually, it was a much more clear-cut situation now that I think about it."

"I never knew that."

"It wasn't something one goes around advertising — especially in those days. For a long time I couldn't talk about it, and then when I could there seemed to be no reason to. It was over."

In the dim light from the living room, Riley's face looks blurred: no wrinkles or lines, just her eyes glowing and her hair like a wiry, silvery halo around her face. "I was going to tell your father the whole story, but when he got old enough to hear it, we weren't close anymore. He had turned into this rather strange, rude young fellow who happened to live here, but with whom I had nothing in common. So I never told him about his father and Lucinda. That was her name. Lucinda. She had long golden hair and very small, rodentlike eyes. I was suspicious of her from the moment I first saw her. They went off to Indiana together."

"Didn't that kill you?"

"Obviously not. However, it did apparently kill your grandfather. He had a heart attack five years later and died."

"I don't think I could bear it if someone I loved ran off with somebody else."

"Maybe you could, and maybe you couldn't."

"I couldn't."

"You do have a choice in the matter, you know. You can die over this terrible thing which has surely happened to about one million other people, or you can get on with your life."

"You make it sound so easy."

"Not easy, Katie. Not easy. *Possible.*"

We swing back and forth, whoosh and creak in the dark, and the air is hot and dry on our faces.

"Remember the summer Robinson was run over?"

She nods. "Of course."

I can close my eyes and still see Robinson by the side of the road, lying there so easy and relaxed, as if he were taking a nap. But I knew he was dead, without knowing what *dead* really meant when it was right there in front of me like that. The outside of Robinson was still there, like a little suit he wore when he was alive. But where was Robinson? Where was the part of Robinson that counted? What would I do without him? Even now I feel like crying when I think about finding him that morning. Riley puts her arm around me and I put my head on her shoulder.

"It was so *unfair.* I thought I'd never stop crying. I woke up crying and went to sleep crying."

"I remember," says Riley.

"And after about a week you told me I had a choice. I could go on feeling sad and terrible or I could start thinking about what a good life Robinson had and all the fun we had with him. Do you remember telling me that?"

"Yes."

"That was the summer you got Yeager and Koufax. You said Robinson was such a special cat it would take two cats to take his place. Remember?"

"I remember."

"And by the end of the summer we could laugh about all the trouble he used to get into. Like the time he got locked up with the Christmas tree. Remember that?"

She laughs. "He threw up tinsel for days."

"And unwrapped the Christmas presents —"

"The cheese! Remember the cheese? Someone had sent us a very grand assortment of cheese, all individually wrapped, and Robinson ate through the tinfoil to get at it. What a mess!"

"Remember how excited he'd get at Easter? He'd scoop jelly beans out of the Easter baskets and hide them —"

"And then the ants would find the jelly beans. What a devil he was. Nothing like Wagner, who's been an angel from the day he was born. Isn't that so, Wagner?" Wagner's tail thumps loudly and for a second he ducks his chin, considering his chain dance. But then he droops his head to his huge paws and looks up at us.

"Remember the candy canes?" I ask.

"What candy canes?"

"The candy canes Wagner ate."

"I think we all imagined the candy cane episode."

"Wagner ate twelve candy canes, and we didn't imagine it because he drooled pink sugar all over your Oriental rug and you were furious."

She laughs again. "It cost a fortune to have it cleaned. I remember, I remember."

I remember.

I like to hear that. *I remember.* Like threads tying everything together, making sense of things.

I can only do this with Riley, because everybody else in my family is so mad at each other. When I talk about things that happened before the divorce, Daddy will say he's forgotten and Mom will say she can't stand to remember.

"That was a long time ago," I say, and we swing slowly in the dark.

"Happy endings belong to fairy tales." Riley's voice is gentle. "But with some luck and hard work you can get a good beginning."

11

It's six-thirty in the morning. The air is hazy and so still I can hear the ships in the harbor. The sun is just coming up over the trees behind the house. Hank's playing solitaire in his pajamas at the kitchen table with Yeager curled up in his lap. From the garden there's the soft hiss of the hose; Riley's already at work, her big gardening hat bobbing between stalks of corn and the green sprawl of tomato plants. Wagner sits underneath the apricot tree scratching a flea.

"You want to play crazy eights?" asks Hank.

"Not right now." I look in the refrigerator and take out a pitcher of orange juice and some cheddar cheese, then get crackers from the cupboard. "Don't you ever get sick of playing cards?"

He looks surprised. "No."

"Wouldn't you like to play Chutes and Ladders or Monopoly or something different once in a while?"

"I don't know. I've never played those games."

"You should try them sometime."

"What are you mad about?"

"Nothing."

"You act mad."

I pour the juice into a glass. "I'm sorry, Hank. I just feel cranky."

"Why?"

"Well, I'm afraid this kidnapping might not change anything."

He nods for a moment, then says, "Your breakfast is all orange."

I look at the juice and cheese and Ritz crackers. "You're right." I open a drawer, searching for a knife to cut the cheese with. "Hank, what am I going to do?"

"The knives are in that drawer over there."

"No, I mean, what am I going to do about my life?"

"What's wrong with it?"

"Everything. Sometimes I think I'm going crazy. Do you ever feel like that?"

He looks at me thoughtfully, his head tilted to one side, as if an answer might come right up out of the floor and he wants to be sure to catch it. Finally he says, "No."

"Never?"

He shakes his head.

"You must have a very nice life, Hank."

"But I've got some problems."

91

"You do?"

"Sometimes."

"Do you like living here?"

He gives me a look that tells me he thinks that's a pretty dumb question. "Where else would I live?"

"Well —"

"Would you like to live here, Kate?"

"Oh, Hank, yes, I'd love to live here. Sometimes I feel I don't really live anywhere at all."

He pats my hand. "You should come live with us."

The doorbell rings. We freeze. Doorbells don't ring at six-thirty in the morning unless something really awful has happened. Or is about to happen.

"Uh-oh," says Hank.

"Who'd be here so early?"

"That policeman."

"You go see who it is. Don't open the door. Just peek through the window. I'll get Riley."

The bell rings again.

"Go on, Hank. It's okay. Don't be scared. I'll get Riley." I run out the back door to the garden. "Riley!" I yell as softly as possible. She can't hear me with the hose on. I have to run up right behind her and tap her on the shoulder.

She gives a little shriek. "Oh! Katie, you startled me. What is it?"

"Somebody's at the front door!"

"How peculiar."

"Do you think it's my parents?"

"Much too soon."

"Maybe it's the police again."

"Well, the thing to do is to be calm." She turns off the water. "And for you to stay out of sight."

Hank comes to the back door. "It's a girl," he calls to us.

"Who is she?" asks Riley.

"She says that she's a friend of Kate's, and her name is Natalie."

"Oh," I groan. Natalie Blanchard, on her way to San Diego. If somebody had said name a million things I could do without right now, Natalie Blanchard would be at the top of my list. I wonder if she brought her fish with her.

"Is she a friend of yours?" asks Riley.

"Well, in a way. Oh, Riley, it's a long story —"

"For heaven's sakes, let's go welcome her."

There's Natalie standing in the front hallway, scarf, Birkenstock sandals, long skirt, and big canvas bag. And yes, in her hand is a McDonald's container. She's brought some of the fish with her.

She's as stunned to see me as I am to see her. "You're in Beverly Hills," she says.

"No, I'm not. I'm in San Pedro. What are *you* doing in San Pedro?"

"This is the big runaway. I'm on my way to San Diego."

Riley holds out her hand. "I'm Riley McAllister and this is Hank." She and Natalie shake hands as if there's nothing unusual about this six-thirty A.M. visit. "Are you hungry, Natalie?"

"Yes."

"Come on in the kitchen and sit down. Kate,

would you get a bowl of cereal for Natalie, please. What do you have in that container? A milk shake?"

"Some fish."

"What kind?"

"A guppy couple. I'm bringing them to my brother."

"Can I see them?" asks Hank.

"Sure." She sets the container on the kitchen table and carefully takes off the lid. Hank looks inside. "The fat plain one is the mother, and the flashy fellow is her husband."

"They're very nice."

"They're okay." Natalie shrugs.

"What kind of cereal would you like?" Riley asks her. "Grape Nuts or Corn Flakes or Cheerios?"

"Doesn't matter."

I put a bowl and a box of Corn Flakes on the table, then get a carton of milk from the refrigerator. Natalie looks up. "Sugar." Nothing polite like "please," just "sugar." I put the sugar bowl in front of her.

"How did you get here?" What I'd really like to ask her is why she's here and when she's leaving.

"Bus," says Natalie.

"A bus from Beverly Hills to San Pedro?"

"It wasn't easy. I had to take three. Three buses. The pits." She takes one of the Corn Flakes and feeds it to her guppies.

"Where do your parents think you are?" Riley sits down across the table from her.

"My father's in San Diego and doesn't think anything yet because he doesn't know I'm on my way.

My mother thinks I'm at my friend Kristin's house."
Natalie looks very relaxed and in charge of the situation. "Why are *you* here?" she asks me.

"I kidnapped her," says Riley.

Natalie looks impressed. "You did?"

"Yes, I did."

"How?"

"Careful planning. You can do anything with enough preparation and planning."

"Exactly!" says Natalie, showing more enthusiasm than I've seen in her during our short acquaintance. "That's how I handled this runaway. That's why my mother thinks I'm at Kristin's house."

"What if she calls and checks?" I ask.

"She won't. What for?"

"To talk to you."

"What about?"

"Well, what if there's an emergency?"

"Kristin will say I'm out."

"Oh."

"See? It's very simple. All good plans are simple."

"How long are you staying here?" I'm almost afraid to hear the answer.

"Don't be rude, Katie," says Riley. "Let Natalie eat her breakfast and then see how she feels. Maybe you ought to stay here overnight, Natalie, and rest up a bit."

Natalie nods. "Thanks."

Why did I ever give Riley's address to Natalie?

"Do you like to play cards?" Hank asks her.

"No. Do you play chess?"

"No."

"I'll teach you. You look smart. I taught my brother when he was your age. I brought my portable chess set with me." She pats her canvas bag next to her chair.

Fritz comes into the kitchen waving the morning paper. "It's on the front page!" he announces.

"This is Natalie," says Hank.

"Hello, Natalie," says Fritz, as if he's accustomed to finding strange girls in the kitchen early in the morning.

"Hello, Fritz," says Natalie. She really was paying attention the other day when I told her all about Riley's house; she knows everybody's name.

Fritz spreads the paper out on the counter. We all crowd around him. And there, right smack in the middle of the front page of the *Los Angeles Times*, are pictures of Daddy and me and a headline that says:

TV STAR'S DAUGHTER MISSING

" 'Beverly Hills police have admitted that television star Michael McAllister's thirteen-year-old daughter, Kate, has been missing from his Beverly Hills home since early yesterday,' " Fritz reads out loud. " 'An investigation is now underway. As yet no ransom demand has been received, and there is speculation that the child's disappearance may be connected with a custody battle between McAllister and his ex-wife, Diana McAllister, who now lives in New York City and who has been unavailable for comment.' "

The *front page*. It feels like that nightmare I sometimes have of walking down the street naked with everybody staring at me. That's what it's like to be on the front page of a newspaper. Naked and embarrassing.

"Your father is not unattractive," says Natalie, looking over my shoulder at the paper. "But you look like you're going to throw up."

"Thanks, Natalie." The picture of me was taken last year in seventh grade and I'm smiling my *TV Guide* smile. Once I read an article in *TV Guide* about girls in beauty contests and how they keep smiling all the time. They press their tongues against the back of their teeth. Maybe it works for them, but it sure didn't work for me. Natalie's right; I look like I'm about to throw up all over the camera.

"You look like your father," says Fritz.

"She's got his eyes," says Riley, "but I think she has her mother's mouth."

"Her father's chin, though." Fritz runs water for the coffeepot.

"Nobody looks like nobody but themselves," says Hank.

"Very wise, Hank." Riley bends down to wipe off his milk mustache.

"What does my father look like?" he asks her.

"I suspect your father is very good-looking."

"But you never met him."

"No, I never met him."

"And my mother's pretty?"

"Very pretty, Hank."

"And really nice?"

"Really nice. And very, very young."

"That's why she had to go away."

"That's right."

"Do you think she'll come back?"

Riley cups Hank's face in her hands and kisses him. "And what do I always say to that?"

Hank shakes his head and smiles. This is a familiar story told over and over. He wants the punch line.

"I hope she doesn't come back!" says Riley. "What would we do without Hank?"

"What would you do without Hank?" he asks.

"Go berserk!"

"And cry a lot?"

"Oceans and oceans of tears. There wouldn't be enough buckets for all our tears!"

"Good." Hank bounces up and down on his toes. "That's good."

Yeager suddenly jumps down from the top of the refrigerator.

"Better cover up your fish," Hank warns Natalie.

"I love cats," she says, putting the lid back on. She reaches for Yeager and then holds him on her lap. "He's very handsome."

"Yes," says Hank. "Is your picture going to be in the paper, too?"

"Not unless I drop dead or something. Even then maybe it won't. I ran away to Catalina once and nobody noticed."

"You do this a lot then?" asks Riley, putting on her gardening gloves.

"All the time. No one pays any attention. But this time is different."

"How?"

"This time I'm going to Jeffrey's house — my father's. That's why I'm going to San Diego. And I'm going to stay. I'm not coming back."

"Well, rest up first. Think about it."

"I have."

"A little more thought never hurt any plan. Kate will show you upstairs. You can share her room," says Riley, taking a few things for granted. She puts on her straw hat. "What else do you do besides run away and keep fish?"

"Lots of stuff. Why?"

"You look like a gypsy. Can you tell fortunes?"

Natalie thinks this over for a minute. "Sure I can tell fortunes. Why?"

"Marvelous. You can come to the party this afternoon and be our fortune-teller." The back door bangs after her.

Natalie looks at me. "Fortunes?"

"Fortunes."

"What am I going to do?"

"You're going to tell fortunes," says Hank.

"Do you know how?" I ask her.

Natalie shakes her head. "No."

"Fritz," I say, "how's Natalie going to learn how to tell fortunes?"

"Research!" he says, getting down his cake-decorating equipment.

"Research, huh?" says Natalie. "What am I going

to do? Find a fortune-teller to interview by this afternoon?"

"Something will turn up," he says, lining everything up neatly on the counter. Fritz is the neatest person I know. It must be from all those years on a ship and not having any room to spread stuff around. He lines up everything in order of appearance in the recipe, and when he's finished, it goes right back to the proper place. Of course he gets very mean and touchy while he's doing this; maybe he'd be happier if he were messy. Maybe I should warn Natalie that he has this Jekyll-and-Hyde problem when he cooks.

"Good morning!" Myra floats into the kitchen in a bright orange dress that has a tiny lace collar. She sees Natalie and smiles. "Why, hello." She doesn't seem surprised to find a perfect stranger in the house first thing in the morning either. She goes over to the cupboards where Fritz is working and looks for a coffee cup.

"Myra, this is —" I start to introduce Natalie to her.

"Out!" shouts Fritz.

"Just a cup for my coffee, Fritz. I won't get in your way."

"Women and children and animals all over the place," he mutters.

I notice Natalie doesn't look amazed or even mildly surprised, just interested. Finally she says, "You're Myra, aren't you? My name is Natalie Blanchard. I'm on my way to San Diego. Do you know anything about fortune-tellers?"

"The library," whispers Myra, then in a normal

voice: "That's what I always told the Randolph girls. If you want to find out about something, go to the library."

"The library," repeats Natalie, nodding. "Is there one close?"

"Not too far, about four blocks."

"I know where it is!" says Hank. "I'll take you."

"Out!" cries Fritz. "I can't decorate this cake with all this noise!"

12

"Fifteen minutes, everybody! Fifteen minutes!" Riley calls from inside the house.

I feel like we're doing a play. One summer Daddy was in a play that toured summer-stock theaters in New England. Every night, backstage, the stage manager would come to his dressing room and knock on the door and call, "Half-hour, Michael!" Then he'd knock again later and call, "Fifteen minutes!" and then, "Five minutes!" and finally, "Places, everyone!" and the curtain would go up. I was very little that summer, and Mom and I were with Daddy for the whole tour — six weeks. We stayed in old summer hotels with white wicker furniture and ceiling fans, and during the day we'd go to beaches or to lakes to swim and lie in the sun. And at night I'd sit in Daddy's dressing room backstage and watch him put on his makeup and his costume. Then he'd give me his watch and ring to wear while he was on stage. It was one of the best times I can remember.

Fritz comes out of the house with part of the puppet stage. He's all dressed up in a blue seersucker suit and is even wearing a bow tie. I finish blowing up a balloon for Hank and then help Fritz carry out the rest of the stage and the box that holds the puppets.

Riley has painted me into a clown — white makeup, a big red grin that goes from ear to ear, eyebrows up to my orange mop wig — I feel like I have frosting on my face. Nobody, not even Mom, would recognize Cat-Man's daughter.

Natalie appears on the porch with her arms outstretched. "Darlinks!" she cries.

"Darlinks?" I look at Fritz and Hank, who don't know what she's talking about either. "What are you saying, Natalie?"

"Dummy! It's my Hungarian fortune-teller accent."

I have never seen a human being wearing as much jewelry as Natalie Blanchard has on her body at this moment. On her ears, her neck, her arms, her fingers — Riley must have dug up everything in the whole house that glittered and shone. Natalie's cheeks are bright with rouge, and she's wearing a lot of green eye shadow and mascara. "Vat do you tink?" she asks, doing a fast little tap-dance step, bracelets and chains and beads clinking and clanking.

"I think you've got a great future as the world's noisiest tap dancer," I tell her. I have mixed emotions about Natalie suddenly being part of Birthday Business.

Austin comes out of the house wearing his cameras, two of them, slung over his shoulders. His thin face looks pale and amazed in the bright sun. He stands squinting at me and Natalie as if trying to figure out just where and how we fit into all of this. Then suddenly he snaps a picture of Natalie waving her arms and rattling her silver bracelets, and then, as I'm still watching him take the picture of Natalie, he whirls around and snaps my picture.

"Austin, that's Natalie," I say, realizing he hasn't met her yet.

"Hello, Austin," says Natalie.

He takes another picture of her.

"Do we have the tape recorder?" calls Riley from the front door.

"It's packed with the puppets," I answer.

"And the cassettes?"

"I'll check."

"Austin, is it your turn to drive?"

Austin nods yes, and takes a picture of Myra coming down the porch steps carrying the party favors. "Oh, Austin," she says. "Don't waste your film."

"Let's get organized!" Fritz stands next to the van and opens up a map. "Does anyone know where we're going?"

"Here's the address." Myra waves a piece of paper.

"You want a map reader?" Natalie jangles and jingles over to the van. "I can read maps. Palms, too. You name it, I can read it. Let's see the address."

104

Riley bends down the brim of her big straw hat to block the sun from her eyes, "Good heavens, it's hot. Did anybody fill Wagner's water bowl?"

"I did," I say.

"Austin," she calls, "we've got to be back in time for the six-o'clock news!"

"Take this road along the ocean . . ." Natalie traces with her finger on the map.

"If we don't get going soon all those rosebuds on my cake are going to melt!" Fritz wipes his forehead with a big white handkerchief.

"Kate, you look splendid!" Myra fusses with my mop wig.

"All the way to this street . . ." Natalie chews her bright red lower lip as she studies the map. "Then we'll turn left and the Haskells are right here, two blocks from the ocean. Got it?"

"Got it," says Austin.

"You probably knew where we were going anyway," says Natalie.

He smiles and shakes his head.

Fritz sits up in front with Austin, the cake on his lap and his banjo balanced between his knees. The rest of us sit in back. As we pull out of the driveway Riley says, "Cake? Puppets? Tape recorder? Balloons? Favors? Camera and film? Banjo?" and after each one the person in charge says, "Yes!"

"Clown and fortune-teller?"

"Yes!" Natalie and I both answer at once.

When my parents and I used to go to the beach, Daddy would do the same thing. "Suntan oil? Towels? Lunch? Reading materials? Frisbee? Sunglasses?" and after he'd called out everything we were supposed to have packed in the car, he'd say, "Child?" and the three of us would laugh even though it wasn't really funny. But it was familiar and expected and ours. Like Hank asking Riley about his parents and wanting to hear the same answers over and over.

I wiggle my toes against the wads of Kleenex stuffed inside the sneakers that are too big for me. The sleeves of Fritz's old jacket cover my hands. The shirt forms a tent over my knees. I feel wonderfully lost inside these clothes. Hidden and secret, yet free. Is this how it feels to be an actor? Is this how my father feels?

Austin has turned on the radio and Rod Stewart is singing about his sexy body.

"Oh, for goodness' sakes, Austin," cries Myra. "Turn that off. There are children in here!"

"That's who likes it. That's who it's *for*!" I yell — loud so I can be heard over Rod Stewart.

"Turn it off or get something else on," Myra yells back. "It's *disgusting*."

Austin punches the buttons on the radio as if he's playing a musical instrument.

Classical music. "Lovely," says Myra. "I believe that's Mozart. That's more like it."

"I don't like this kind of music," says Hank, who's holding on to about thirty balloons.

Austin pushes another button. News. "The temperature at the Civic Center in Los Angeles today is ninety-two degrees —"

Everyone is yelling now.

"Mozart!"

"Austin, keep your eyes on the road!"

"The cake's going to melt!"

"I want to hear the news!"

"Mozart!"

"Just turn the thing off," says Riley.

Sudden silence. The radio is off.

And then Riley starts to laugh, then Fritz and Myra and Hank and Natalie. We're all laughing, even Austin.

I love this. Right now. The hot bright afternoon, the road that winds and dips next to the blue ocean, feeling excited about the party, everybody laughing — I wish this moment could go on forever.

The rabbit sits in the middle of the Haskells' kitchen.

"That's Heathcliff," says Mrs. Haskell.

"He lives inside the house," says Holly Haskell. "He has a kitty-litter box."

"Does he use it?" asks Natalie.

"Sometimes." Holly is dressed as a nurse, which I guess is what she wants to be when she grows up. She's wearing a white dress, a nurse's cap, white stockings, and even white shoes.

"Heathcliff doesn't like parties," says Holly's brother, who looks like he's about my age and is chewing bubble gum and making it crack. "Parties make him weird." He turns to me and says, "Are you a real clown?"

I nod.

"Prove it."

"Craig, go ride your bike or something," says

Mrs. Haskell, who's wearing sneakers and a tennis dress. Holly's nurse's uniform looks like one of her mother's tennis dresses with some tucks taken in it.

Hank pets Heathcliff, and the rabbit thumps loudly with his hind foot, his nose going up and down and his whiskers vibrating.

"You see," says Craig. "He's getting weird. I told you, he hates parties."

Riley comes into the Haskells' kitchen carrying the box of puppets. "Is that a rabbit under the table?"

"What's in the box?" asks Craig.

"Magic," says Riley. "I adore rabbits. What's this fellow's name?"

"Heathcliff."

"Hello, Heathcliff." She bends down and peers at him closely. Heathcliff's pink nose twitches. "He's a very handsome rabbit. Now — where shall we set up the puppet stage? Natalie, you come with me, please."

"I thought we'd have the puppets in the family room," says Mrs. Haskell. "Right through that door over there."

Fritz carefully takes the birthday cake out of the box and sets it on the kitchen table. It's a long rectangular cake, covered with pink frosting and dozens of fragile, beautiful rosebuds, and in the middle: HAPPY BIRTHDAY TO HOLLY, written in swirly strokes.

"Oh, what a magnificent cake!" cries Mrs. Haskell.

Fritz makes a dignified little bow.

"What time is it?" asks Holly.

"Ten more minutes, dear," says Mrs. Haskell.

"When will Daddy get home?"

"Soon."

Austin snaps a picture of Holly drumming her fingers on the kitchen table, staring at Fritz's beautiful cake.

Myra unpacks the favors and prizes. "Has anybody seen Hank?" I shake my head, remembering I'm not supposed to talk. "Go find him and see if he's put the balloons on the mailbox," says Myra.

He's helping Riley, Fritz, and Natalie set up the puppet stage. "Balloons on mailbox?" I whisper in his ear.

"I forgot." He picks up a half-dozen balloons and heads for the front door, then turns and smiles at me. "Isn't this fun?"

I nod up and down very fast.

In the kitchen Austin is still snapping pictures of Holly. "One with the rabbit?" he says.

Holly tries to pick up Heathcliff, but he gives another thump with his hind foot and hops behind the refrigerator. "Come out of there right now, Heathcliff!" she yells. "Come on, don't you want to be in my birthday picture, you dumb rabbit?"

"Maybe the clown?" suggests Austin.

I stand behind Holly's chair and look at the camera. I usually hate having my picture taken, but I have this feeling that this new me with makeup and funny clothes is free and not afraid of anything.

13

The doorbell rings and the guests start to arrive. There's another nurse, a baseball player wearing her Little League uniform, and an astronaut. Those are the ones I can figure out. There's also a girl wearing a black leotard with plastic flowers pinned all over it from her neck right down to her feet. Another girl wears an apron and a little papoose on her back with a Baby Tender Love in it. She's also wearing boots and a cowboy hat. Another wears a long skirt, a hat with feathers on it, jewelry, false eyelashes, and jogging shoes.

Each time the doorbell rings and a new guest arrives, the kids scream and squeal. Riley takes charge right away so they don't all go berserk. She holds a big jar of jelly beans, and everybody has to calm down enough to guess how many jelly beans there are.

"A hundred and eight, a hundred and nine, a hundred and ten . . ." The baseball player is counting them.

"You're not supposed to count them, Caroline. You're supposed to *guess*," says the astronaut, who's wearing part of a vacuum-cleaner hose. "Caroline is *counting*. This is going to take forever if Caroline counts all the jelly beans."

"You can't count them," says a nurse. "You can't see the ones in the middle. How can Caroline count the ones in the middle? See what I mean?"

"A hundred and eighteen, a hundred and nineteen," counts Caroline.

"That's *cheating*," says the girl with all the flowers pinned to her leotard. "Stop cheating, Caroline!"

"What happens when you win?" asks Baby Tender Love's mother.

"You win the jelly beans," says Riley.

Natalie and I write down everyone's guess on a pad of paper and answer the door. The last guest to arrive is dressed like a tube of Crest toothpaste.

"You wanna be toothpaste when you grow up, Betsy?" asks the astronaut. *"Toothpaste?"*

"A dentist, dummy."

"You want to be a *dentist*?" asks Holly.

"How many jelly beans?" Riley asks Crest toothpaste.

Crest toothpaste circles awkwardly around the jar a couple of times and thinks. "Two hundred and twenty," she says.

Natalie writes it down. Everyone has guessed the number of jelly beans except for Caroline, who is still counting. Austin takes a picture of her pulling on her baseball cap and squinting at the jar.

"There are one hundred and eighty-two jelly beans in the jar," says Caroline finally.

Riley pulls a sealed envelope out of her pocket and hands it to me. "And the winner is . . ."

I open the envelope and hold up the card inside. On it, written in big figures, is the number 184.

"Caroline wins," says Natalie. "She's got the closest guess."

"That's not fair!" says a nurse. "She cheated. She counted!"

"You could have counted if you wanted to," says Caroline.

Riley hands her the jar of jelly beans and announces that it's time to open the presents.

In the family room everybody sits down in a circle around Holly and the big pile of presents.

"Oh, Caroline, I love it!" screams Holly. "I just *love* it!" She holds up the present for everyone to see and there are more screams. I feel like screaming myself. It's a Cat-Man doll, the grossest doll in the whole world. It's a cat covered with fake fur and there's this little zipper hidden on the cat's back. You unzip the cat and inside there's a miniature Cat-Man who's wearing blue jeans and a plaid shirt. His little plastic face is orange, and even though it's orange and made out of plastic, it looks just like Daddy.

"Oh, I've been wanting one!" cries Holly.

"I love Cat-Man," says Caroline.

"He's so *cute*," says Crest toothpaste.

"Did you hear about his daughter?"

"Yes!"

"What about his daughter?"

"She's been kidnapped."

"You're *kidding!*"

"It's true. It was in the paper this morning. Don't you read the paper?"

"He doesn't look old enough to have a daughter that old."

"How old is she?"

"Older than us. About thirteen, I think."

I'm holding my breath. I feel like I'm invisible. My face must be bright red under the white makeup. Hank and Natalie are on either side of me, and they both move closer until we're all pressed together.

"I hope they don't kill her."

"I bet Cat-Man will figure it out."

"He's an *actor*. He's not really Cat-Man."

"Well, I bet he knows lots of tricks about how to catch crooks. Just from pretending to be Cat-Man he must have learned something."

"Crooks don't have her. They think her mother kidnapped her!"

"Girls! The fortune-teller will read your palms right after the presents are all opened. And the puppet show will begin in fifteen minutes," Riley announces.

"Oh, wait — there's another present!" says Holly. She unwraps it and then screams, "Oh! How wonderful! Oh, Betsy, thank you!" She holds up a giant candy bar.

"Open it, Holly, let's eat it!"

"What kind of a dentist gives a present like that?" asks Caroline.

"What do you know?" says Crest toothpaste.

"I know it's about a million cavities!"

A tall man with freckles and red hair stands in the doorway, holding a huge package wrapped in pink ribbons. "Daddy!" cries Holly, jumping up and flinging her arms around him.

Natalie is taking this fortune-teller business very seriously. She looks at Holly's palm first. Everybody giggles. The more serious Natalie gets, the more nervous they get, and the more they giggle.

"Oh, *good*," says Natalie, bending over Holly's hand.

Holly stops giggling. "Why did you say, 'Oh, good'?"

"You have a long life line. This being your birthday and everything, it would have been embarrassing if you didn't."

"You could've lied," says Caroline.

Natalie gives Caroline a look that could cut down trees. "Fortune-tellers never lie."

I just hope she doesn't find somebody with a lousy life line and ruin the party by telling her the bad news. At least she's dropped her Hungarian-fortune-teller accent.

"Ah," she says.

"What?" Holly looks anxious. "Why did you say 'Ah' like that?"

"You are careless of personal property and your own safety."

"That's true," says the astronaut. "She broke her arm roller-skating last spring. Then she lost her roller skates."

"How do you know that?" Holly asks Natalie. "You're guessing."

Natalie rattles her bracelets and points to some lines in Holly's palm. "Your line of life and line of the head don't begin together. That's always an indication of carelessness."

"Oh," says Holly.

Everyone has stopped giggling.

Craig is sitting under the piano in the corner. Every once in a while he gets a little piece of wrapping paper that Hank and I have missed, rolls it into a ball, and shoots it at one of the guests.

"Cut that out, Craig," says Mr. Haskell, but he doesn't sound mean or mad about it.

Banjo music comes from behind the puppet stage. Everybody quiets down and turns to face the stage. Hank carries a basket of paper and ribbons up to the kitchen. Austin crouches next to the stage, facing the guests and Holly, his camera ready. The draperies are closed so that the room is almost dark as we all wait for the show to start.

Hank taps me on the back. "Go see Myra," he whispers in my ear. "There's a problem."

"A problem?"

Hank nods. "A bad one." His mouth is stretched back as if he's just seen a disaster or eaten something really disgusting.

"What kind of a problem?"

"A bad kind."

The curtains are opening for the puppet show. "Okay," I say, and reluctantly go to see what Myra's problem is.

Myra is standing in the middle of the kitchen. Only her eyes move when I come in, as if whatever's gone wrong is so awful she has frozen into one position with shock.

"What is it, Myra?"

She shakes her head slowly back and forth. "A tragedy has occurred."

"*What* tragedy?"

She doesn't answer. She just points.

Pink icing. Everywhere. Little blobs of pink icing all over the kitchen.

"Is that what I think it is?"

"Yes! Fritz's cake."

"Who —"

"That little beast. That Hemingway or Hathaway or whatever it is they call him. That *rodent.*"

"Heathcliff," I say, beginning to realize the full extent of this tragedy. "How did he get into it?"

"He jumped up on that chair and then right onto the table and into the cake. He's hiding behind the refrigerator now."

Sure enough, there's Heathcliff behind the refrigerator looking like a candy rabbit. Like the Easter Bunny himself. Pink frosting clings to his whiskers and covers his ears, and he looks like he's wearing pink booties.

"Does Fritz know?"

"Of course not," says Myra. "You know what's going to happen when Fritz finds out."

"A second tragedy."

"He'll murder the rabbit. I just know he will. Then our business will go right down the drain. Who would hire people for children's birthday parties who end up killing the family pet?"

"You're absolutely right, Myra." I look at the smashed birthday cake on the table. "We've got to do something."

"Of course we've got to do something! But *what*?"

"I'm thinking."

"Who ever thought a rabbit would do such a thing?"

"Riley will know what to do."

"But we can't interrupt her in the middle of the puppet show. Fritz would get suspicious."

"But we've got to do something!"

"That's what I've been telling you!"

"Look, Myra. It's their rabbit, right? I mean, in a way this is the Haskells' problem, isn't it?"

"But what difference does that make? You know what Fritz will do no matter whose problem it is. And we're supposed to have a birthday cake. We don't have one."

We're talking in circles. I'm even walking in circles as I try to think what to do. Outside the kitchen window I see a boy's bike propped up against the garage. A very simple, obvious plan pops into my head. "Myra, I'm going to buy another cake."

"How? Where?"

"We passed some stores about a mile away. There was a little shopping center with a fountain. There's a bike outside and it won't take me more than fifteen minutes. I'll get a cake and one of those little tubes

117

of frosting, and we can write Holly's name on it. Meanwhile, think of a way to keep Fritz calm about all this."

"Are you going like that?" she asks.

"Like what?" I look down and notice my hands are lost in the sleeves of Fritz's jacket. I'm a clown. "Well, so what? Somebody's got to go get the cake. Can you ride a bike?"

"I've never ridden one."

"Okay, so I'll go get the cake. Do you have any money?"

She gets a ten-dollar bill out of her purse.

"How much time do I have?" I stuff the money into the pocket of my baggy jeans.

She looks at the kitchen clock. "The puppet show will last about ten minutes more, and then there will be games for fifteen minutes."

"I've got plenty of time then. You do something about Fritz."

"I *can't*. I just don't have the nerves for Fritz's temper."

"Tell Natalie to do it. She can handle him."

"Good luck."

"Good luck to Natalie!"

Some boys pass me in a sports car with the top down, and one yells, "Hey, Halloween isn't until October!"

I just keep pumping up the hill, concentrating on that cake. No matter how embarrassing this gets, it's still a lot easier than telling Fritz that a rabbit jumped into his cake. I wonder how Natalie will handle it. I feel a little bit guilty for dumping that job on her.

Another car passes me and honks. The woman driving smiles at me and I honk the bike horn back. Natalie's pretty tough, though. She's not going to be afraid of Fritz's temper. My emotions aren't mixed anymore about Natalie being part of Birthday Business.

Two joggers run by and I honk the horn again. They laugh and wave at me. Riding through town in broad daylight dressed like a clown isn't exactly the easiest thing in the world, either.

Some girls come roller-skating down the street and point at me and giggle. A man watering his lawn sees me and waves. "Hi!" he calls in a friendly voice. I wave back at him. The neat green lawns flash past me. I imagine that music from *Rocky* is playing. Everybody cheering Kate the Great Clown.

And then finally up ahead there's a fountain and the small group of stores, and right on the corner is a grocery store. I park the bike in a rack by the door. I've been pedaling so hard and fast that my legs are shaking when I get off, and my clothes, or rather Fritz's clothes, are damp and sticking to me. I take a deep breath and go into the store.

"Well, look at *that*!" cries a woman pushing a shopping cart filled to the top with groceries. "What are you *doing*?"

I make a deep bow and hurry down an aisle looking for the bakery section. Cereals, vegetables, fruit juice, and finally, bread, rolls, pies, and *cakes*. There are two chocolate cakes, one with yellow frosting and one with white.

A little girl, very little, about three years old, pulls on my sleeve. "Hi," she says.

I reach down and shake her hand.

I decide on the white cake. But where do they keep those little tubes of frosting? I look at the clock over the front of the store. The puppet show has already ended and they're playing games now. Up and down the aisles — the little girl follows me, then her little brother joins us. People stop their carts to stare at me. Some of them look confused. Finally, flour, sugar, and *frosting* — mixes, cans, and tubes. I grab a tube of pink frosting and run to the checkout counter. There are three people ahead of me in line. I check the clock again. Eight minutes.

"A clown?" I hear a girl behind me say to a friend.

"Yeah, it's a clown. What do you know, a clown."

"What a dumb thing to do. Going shopping dressed up like a clown. Is it a boy clown or girl clown?"

"I can't tell."

"Now I've seen everything. A clown grocery shopping."

Don't they realize clowns have ears?

The man checking groceries is round and smiling and wearing a big white apron. "You look like you've run away from the circus!" he says. I nod and hand him the rumpled ten-dollar bill. "A runaway clown?" he asks in a stage whisper. I nod again. He winks and hands me my change. "Good luck!"

Myra and Natalie are watching out the kitchen window for me.

"They just this minute finished the games!" says Myra. "Do you have the cake?"

I hand her the bag. "Does Fritz know?"

"Sure," says Natalie. "I told him."

She looks so calm and cool. "You did?"

"Yes."

"Didn't he have a fit?"

"He adjusted before I told him."

"How? What do you mean?"

"I read his palm while the games were going on. I told him tragedy was right around the corner. He wanted to know what kind of tragedy. Was it an early grave? He was very upset. I said I had no idea what the tragedy would be, but that it would be a real biggie. Then five minutes later I told him not to worry. The tragedy had already happened but was relatively minor. When he found out it was only a rabbit in his cake, he was relieved."

14

"**H**urry up, girls!" Riley gets a white bowl down from the cupboard for the popcorn. "We don't want to miss the news. It's almost six."

Natalie stirs the melting butter. "That party was fun."

"I don't know what we'd have done without you two. If you ever need a job as a fortune-teller, give me a call," says Riley.

"I certainly will."

I line up root-beer glasses on a tray. "The Haskells reminded me a little bit of Shannon's family."

"Who's Shannon?" asks Natalie.

"My best friend in New York. She's got a terrific family."

"Why?"

"What do you mean — *why*?"

"What makes them so terrific?"

"Well, for one thing they're normal."

"What's 'normal'?" Natalie asks, and takes the butter off the stove. Yeager's watching the popcorn maker like it's alive and ought to be caught.

"Normal's the way things are supposed to be," I tell Natalie, who for a smart girl can be awfully dumb sometimes.

"Oh. *Boring*."

"It doesn't sound boring to me." I dish scoops of vanilla ice cream into the root-beer glasses.

"Your parents certainly don't sound boring."

"I know. I wish they were."

"Five minutes until the news, girls." Riley unplugs the popcorn maker and fills the bowl with the popcorn.

Natalie pours butter over it. "Do you have popcorn and root-beer floats for dinner often?"

"Only when Riley cooks."

"I think cooking is a waste of time," says Riley. "Hurry up with the floats, Katie. You get the napkins, Natalie."

"Good evening," says Kelly Lange of Channel Four News. "Kate McAllister, daughter of television star Michael McAllister, has been missing since early yesterday from her father's home in Beverly Hills and is believed to have been kidnapped. McAllister, star of the ABC hit series *Cat-Man*, told police he is convinced that his daughter was taken by her mother, Diana McAllister of New York City. Susan Hahn is standing by with a live News Center Four report frow Beverly Hills. Susan —"

"The lead story, no less!" says Myra.

"Shh," says Fritz.

And there's Daddy, looking madder than I've ever seen him, standing in front of his house with Susan Hahn. He looks even madder than when I t.p.-ed the whole front of his house last summer. Jessica is standing behind him, bouncing up and down, looking frantic but at the same time sort of thrilled.

"Who's that?" asks Riley.

"His new girlfriend. Her name's Jessica." I'm getting that nightmare feeling again of walking down the street naked.

"I woke up about three o'clock yesterday morning," Daddy's saying. "My housekeeper was playing the flute."

"Playing the flute," Susan Hahn repeats, as if flute playing wakes up a lot of people at three in the morning these days.

"Thank goodness he doesn't suspect Christina of being part of this!" whispers Myra.

"Did you discover your daughter was missing then?" asks Susan Hahn.

Big close-up of Daddy. He pushes his hair out of his eyes. "Ms. Wald went to wake my daughter at nine when she didn't come down for breakfast," he says, and I'm wondering — who's Ms. Wald?

So is Susan Hahn, because she asks, "Ms. Wald is your housekeeper?"

"No, Ms. Wald is a friend." He turns to Jessica and she gives a shaky smile.

"Is it possible," asks Susan Hahn, "knowing the difficult court battle you and your former wife went through for custody of your daughter, that she might be involved in your daughter's disappearance?"

"Is it *possible*?" repeats Daddy, his voice booming out of the television set. "It's not possible — it's a *fact*! Her mother's got her. Her mother kidnapped her!"

"You're going to be famous after this," says Natalie. "Next you'll be doing talk shows."

"That's not funny."

She gives a shrug. "Who's trying to be funny?"

And then Kelly Lange is back saying, "Diana McAllister, former wife of Michael 'Cat-Man' McAllister and mother of their missing thirteen-year-old daughter Kate, arrived in Los Angeles just hours ago. Paul Dandridge was there."

Riley gives me a poke.

And now Mom in living color. She's wearing dark glasses and jeans, a red T-shirt, and Cherokee sandals. She's hurrying down the tunnellike passageway at the airport with Paul Dandridge and his microphone and all the camera equipment trying to keep up with her.

"Mrs. McAllister, have you heard the accusations your former husband had made?"

"I've heard them!" Mom is not going to pretend she's in a good mood just because she's on television. She's a very tough lady.

"Why do you think he's accusing you —"

"*Why*?" Mom stops suddenly and whirls around. All the people behind her, including Paul Dandridge, bump into each other. "I'll tell you why! *He* has her! This is a plot he's cooked up! And you want to know something else?"

For a second there's no sound and people are still bumping into each other, and then the camera gets

125

bumped and goes out of control with close-ups of strangers and Paul Dandridge's feet, then back to Mom, who is now shaking her fist at him.

"He's not going to get away with it!" Mom yells. "I'm going to find her!"

I have to admit Mom is no wimp.

The camera cuts to Paul Dandridge, who speaks very low and fast like he's going to duck out of there and disappear the minute he's off camera. "Los Angeles International Airport. News Center Four. Paul Dandridge reporting."

"I like a woman with spunk," says Fritz.

"What's going to happen when that lady finds out Cat-Man doesn't have Kate?" asks Hank.

"That, my darling boy, is the sixty-four-thousand-dollar question," says Riley, and bends over to wipe Hank's buttery chin.

It's the Cat-Man and Bunny show. I think it's great Mom's not afraid of anybody or anything and comes charging out here to rescue me — I just wish she didn't have to be so *public* about it. I wish she could be tough in private. I don't like being the big story on the evening news; I just want to be an average person everybody leaves alone. It's okay for Daddy to be famous, that's his business, but I don't want to be famous.

Out of Natalie's big canvas bag come five Harlequin romances, a portable chess set, tap shoes, a framed photograph of a little boy ("Is that Dwight?" I ask. "No, it's the President of the United States," says Natalie), a bag of sunflower seeds, fish food, more skirts and Danskin tops, and some scarves.

I sit on my bed and watch her unpack all this stuff to get to a nightgown. "Isn't that kind of heavy to carry around?" I ask.

"I've got strong arms," says Natalie, finding a toothbrush at the bottom of the bag. Her arms look like pale toothpicks.

The weather is turning cool. I find two light blankets at the top of the closet and toss one on her bed. The dry, grassy smell of the Santa Ana is gone and the air feels heavy.

Natalie takes off her scarf and brushes her hair. "I like Riley a lot," she says.

"Good."

"What's wrong with you tonight?"

"Nothing."

"Nothing?"

"That's right. Nothing." I put on a nightgown that fit me three summers ago. "What time are you leaving tomorrow?"

"Ten. Riley's taking me to the bus station in Long Beach. I can get a Greyhound bus straight to San Diego."

"Is your father meeting you?"

"How could he do that? He doesn't know I'm coming. It's going to be a big surprise."

"Maybe you ought to let him know — just in case."

"Just in case of what?" She stops brushing her hair and looks at me.

"Well, in case they're busy or something."

"I'm not going down for the weekend. I'm going down to stay. It doesn't matter if they're busy. There's time now."

"But if they're busy, they won't be able to come to the bus station to pick you up."

"I'll take another bus out to their house then."

I tuck the blanket around my bed. "I love buses."

"What's to love about a bus?"

"Well, not the bus itself exactly, what I love is riding on them."

"You're kidding." Natalie stretches out on the floor and starts to do sit-ups.

"No, I'm serious. Shannon and I take buses all the time in New York."

"Where to?"

"Not really *to* anyplace — just around New York. Down to Greenwich Village and Chinatown. All over. Sometimes we don't even get off. It's fun."

"Why?"

"There's always something happening."

"Nothing ever happens in Beverly Hills," says Natalie, not the slightest bit out of breath from all these sit-ups she's doing. "At least not outside where you can see it happen."

"Stuff happens all the time in New York. People make speeches, go crazy, sing, tap-dance — right out on the street." I get into bed and smooth the sheet and blanket so all the wrinkles disappear. Natalie's head keeps bobbing up and down between the beds. "Are you excited about tomorrow?"

"Excited about tomorrow?" she repeats, looking puzzled.

"About seeing Dwight and your father . . ."

She stops doing sit-ups and thinks for a minute. "Yeah," she finally says. "Kind of. But if you don't expect much, you don't get disappointed."

128

"But it'll be like having a normal family. Do you like your stepmother?"

"She's okay."

"You're lucky to have a brother."

"So are you."

"Huh?"

"You've got Hank."

"Well, Hank's wonderful and I love him very much, but —"

"But what?"

"He's not a *real* relative."

"So what?" Natalie stands up and gives me a disgusted look.

"Hank's not my real brother."

"So *what?*"

"Look, Natalie —"

"*You* look! You're so dumb I don't believe it. What's a real brother anyway? What difference does it make if you have the same parents? I don't love Dwight just because we have the same parents. We have lousy parents! I love him *in spite of* having the same lousy parents. He's my friend."

"Hank's my friend, too, but —"

"But *what?* You make me sick, Kate McAllister. You make me so sick I could barf! All this whining about wanting a normal family. You've got a family, a *real* family, but you're too dumb to know it. You've got Riley and all the people in this house. You've got a home here is what you've got, dummy. And your grandmother loves you so much she does something really crazy like kidnapping you! What more do you want?"

I just stare at her, not knowing what to say.

"I feel like I live in a TV series," she says, "and it's always being canceled. You want to know how many places I've lived in? *Forty-six*. I figured it out once. Forty-six different rooms, and that includes hotel rooms we lived in for over a month. And you've had this room waiting here for you all of your life and you're complaining because you don't have this normal boring family of your dreams. You really make me *sick!* She grabs her nightgown and goes into the bathroom, slamming the door so hard behind her that the whole room rattles.

My thoughts back up and bump against each other, making so much noise I can't make sense out of them. The water runs and runs in the bathroom. I wonder if I really did make her barf. Or maybe she's in there crying. I can't imagine Natalie crying. Do I really whine all the time about a normal family? Is this my real family right here in this house? Maybe real families aren't always normal families.

15

Fritz has cooked a special breakfast for Natalie — French toast, sausages, and juice he just squeezed from the oranges in the garden.

"We're going to miss you," says Riley.

"Yeah?" says Natalie.

"Yes, and the party this afternoon won't be the same without a fortune-teller. Don't forget to call me if you want a job."

"I'll keep that in mind," she says in her cool, flat voice, but she's smiling.

Even Austin comes down to say good-bye to her. He doesn't actually say good-bye or anything conventional like that, he just looks at her, his head tilted to one side.

"See you around, Austin," she says.

"Will you send me a postcard from San Diego?" asks Hank.

"Sure I will."

"Kate sends me postcards all the time from New York."

"She does, huh?" Natalie looks at me and sips her juice.

I want to tell her that a lot of what she said last night made sense, but I'm not really sure how to say anything serious to Natalie. She might laugh at me.

At the front door, juggling the fish, she dips into her canvas bag and pulls out the portable chess set. "Here," she says, handing it to Hank. "Get Kate to play with you." Then she looks me straight in the eye and says, "You were right. The bag's too heavy."

Riley toots the horn for Natalie to hurry up. Wagner sticks his head out of the back of the van and barks.

" 'Bye, Natalie."

" 'Bye, Kate." She slips something into my hand and flies down the porch steps. The rest of us wave good-bye until they back out of the driveway and disappear down the street.

I open my hand. Her silver earrings. I feel an awful lump in my throat as I put them on and look at myself in the hallway mirror. I look different in them. They swing and glitter, and I like the feeling they give me. I show them to Myra.

"That Natalie is a very special girl," she says. "I hope everything works out for her in San Diego."

"I do, too."

It's a warm, soupy morning. The sky is thick and hazy, the air is damp.

"You want to try to play chess with me?" asks Hank.

"Not right now. Later."

When I go into the den and get the photograph album out of the bookcase, Myra feels my forehead with her cool, dry hand. "You look a little peaked," she says.

"I'm all right." I leaf through the album. There are pictures of Riley when she moved into this house. The house, surrounded by tiny, thin trees and short shrubs, looks bare and too new. Riley, her hair long and darker, wearing bright clothes, laughs into the camera. There are pictures of my grandfather, who doesn't look like the sort of man who would run away with someone named Lucinda to Indiana. He's wearing a hat and a striped suit with a vest, and he seems embarrassed and impatient with the camera. He looks narrow and proper. There's Daddy when he was my age, sitting on the front steps of this house, his arms around a dog that looks just like Wagner. Natalie's earrings brush against my cheeks as I bend over the album. I feel like the heavy gray sky is pressing down on top of me. I hope everything is going to be okay for Natalie. I keep hearing the stuff she said to me last night going around and around in my head like a record.

I go up to the attic and watch Austin paint for a while. Sometimes Austin is my favorite person to be with because I don't have to answer any questions or explain what I'm thinking or feeling. He just accepts me. He's working on a painting of circles. Circles within circles within circles. His paintings are like him — you can't put them into words.

* * *

"Now, pay attention so you can do this yourself," says Riley, as if I'll be doing a lot more parties with them.

I try not to move my mouth as she spreads white makeup over my chin. "You know what Natalie said to me last night?"

"What did she say?"

"That I should stop whining about wanting a normal family because I've already got a *real* family. Right here."

"Natalie's a smart girl."

"I mean, everybody here loves each other even though they fight sometimes. And Austin can stay up in the attic and everybody understands, and when Fritz is cranky in the kitchen nobody really minds. Nobody has to pretend anything around here. Maybe that's what a family is all about. Just being yourself and loving each other no matter what happens."

Riley just nods and draws on my clown eyebrows.

"Would you want me here? I mean, all the time?"

"Oh, Katie, what kind of a foolish question is that? You know I would."

What would my parents say to *that*? If Natalie can be so independent and take charge of her own life, why can't I? "You're sure?" I ask.

"More than anything else in the world, I'd like to have you live here."

Hank and I sit on the stairs in the front hallway blowing up balloons for the party. He ties the ends of the strings to Wagner's collar.

"Don't you think all those balloons make him nervous?" I ask.

"No. Wagner likes balloons," says Hank. "Nothing makes Wagner nervous."

The sun has finally burned through the haze of this morning, and long strips of sunlight shine through the front door across the hall. Yeager and Koufax are stretched out above us, each on his own step, paws dangling down.

In the kitchen Fritz plays the banjo and sings, "A penny for a spool of thread, a penny for a needle . . ."

Upstairs, Riley is rehearsing Peter Pan for the puppet show for today's party. "How clever I am!" she sings in Peter's voice, and then begins to crow. Then stops and does it over and over again. She's not happy with the way she crows.

Myra's in the den listening to Melinda decide between Roger and a newcomer named Dennis.

"You want to play chess?" asks Hank.

"Okay." I'm trying not to scratch my nose, which is covered with white makeup.

Hank blows up one more balloon to replace the one Wagner has just popped, then sets up the portable chess set, which he's got right there with him. He does it very slowly and carefully. "Natalie taught this to me last night."

"You've got the bishops and the knights reversed."

He switches them and then stares at the board. "Hmm."

A car pulls into the driveway, spattering gravel, and *skreetch*ing to a stop.

Hank and I look at each other. "Police?" he whispers, his eyes wide and scared looking.

All I can do is shake my head. It's not the police.

Footsteps clatter up to the porch — and there they are.

Mom and Daddy.

Together.

Here in San Pedro.

This is what we've been waiting for, *expecting*. Why am I in a state of shock?

They open the screen door and step over Wagner. They're both wearing blue jeans and T-shirts. They look like such *ordinary* people. They're looking at me, puzzled, as if they've met me somewhere but can't recall my name.

"Pop goes the weasel!" sings Fritz in the kitchen. Upstairs Peter Pan crows. Wagner jumps up all covered with balloons and tries to do his chain dance. In the den, Melinda wails, *"It's no good Roger, it never was."*

"Hi, Mom," I say, my voice high and squeaky. "Hi, Daddy."

"Oh, my God," cries Mom. "That clown is Kate!"

16

The way I say good-bye is like this: I say, "See you soon," even though I'm going to fly three thousand miles away and won't see someone for months or a year or who knows when. I always say, "See you soon," like I'm just going around the corner for a loaf of bread. Very casual and cool. It's the same trick that Natalie uses.

Now I say, "See you soon," to everybody on the front porch. I try not to think of them as a family — real, mine, or any kind. This is just a bunch of people I visit once in a while. I give Myra a hug, then Austin, who surprises me and hugs me back, and Fritz, who's so gruff and tough but smells of vanilla and sugar and kisses me on the forehead, and then Hank, who buries his face in my neck and makes it wet when I bend down to kiss him.

I think Riley knows this trick about being cool. "Take care, Katie," she says, smiling.

"See you soon," I say.

"Yes," and she kisses me and hugs me close.

"Well, I'm not going to say a word," says Mom when we're in the car, heading for Beverly Hills.

Sitting between my parents in the front seat, I can feel Daddy tense up the minute Mom opens her mouth. We're on the freeway now, and he's driving very fast.

"The speed limit is fifty-five, you know," says Mom.

He doesn't answer.

"Well!" Mom can't stand silence for more than about one minute. She pats my leg. "At least you're safe and sound. Since I'm here I might as well spend the weekend. Besides, your father's week isn't up yet. I thought we'd take the red-eye back to New York Sunday night. How does that sound?"

"Okay." The red-eye is a plane that leaves Los Angeles late at night and gets to New York at dawn. Everybody on it is so tired they've got red eyes.

"You've still got some of that white stuff on your face." Mom gets a tissue from her purse and dabs at my neck. "I don't understand Riley," she mutters. "I just don't understand her."

"It was simply a crazy idea," says Daddy.

"Simply a crazy idea?" Mom's voice goes up an octave. "Riley mobilized the entire Beverly Hills police force! She made our family's personal problems into a media event! She made me leave my office to fly three thousand miles, and heaven only knows what effect this will all have on Kate —"

I sit up straight and try to look alert and healthy to show it's had a very positive effect on me.

"And that houseful of weirdos —" Mom goes on. "She's running a hangout for fruitcakes down there."

"They're her family," I explain.

"Her *family!* Oh, now I've heard everything. She's always had peculiar people living in her house. Michael, remember when we got married, there was that fellow she found on the dock who thought he was the Lone Ranger?"

"The Pied Piper," says Daddy.

"I don't remember the Pied Piper being there."

"No, the fellow didn't think he was the Lone Ranger, he thought he was the Pied Piper. You've forgotten his clarinet."

"See?"

"Look, Diana. Everything's fine now, okay? Kate is safe."

"But what kind of a person *steals a child?*" And then with an awful gulp she starts to cry. "Oh, Katie, I was so worried about you."

"Oh, Mom . . ."

"Now Diana, take it easy." Daddy reaches over and touches her hand, then starts to fiddle with the radio. Nobody says anything while Mom sniffs, gets another Kleenex out of her purse, and blows her nose.

"What do you know about Natalie Blanchard?" Daddy suddenly asks me.

"Natalie Blanchard?" My heart pounds. Life has really gotten complicated lately. "Not much. Why?"

"Do you know where she is?"

I concentrate on pulling a thread out of the frayed bottoms of my shorts. "She's in San Diego," I say very softly, as if the softer I say it, the less it counts. "She's gone to live with her father and little brother."

"Is Riley involved in this?" Mom asks.

"Not really —"

"What do you mean, *not really*?"

"Well, Natalie kind of stopped by on her way to San Diego. She spent the night at Riley's."

"See?" Mom leans across me and looks at Daddy. "See?"

"See *what*?"

"Riley was involved!" Mom blows her nose again. "I'm not going to say another word about this, Michael. Not another word."

He looks relieved.

One thing is certain. This is not the time to announce that I want to live with Riley.

"How did you know Natalie was missing?" I ask.

"Her mother called me," says Daddy.

"Natalie told her mother she was staying at a friend's house," says Mom, "and her mother met the friend's mother at Saks yesterday and discovered Natalie wasn't staying with them. She says Natalie does this a lot. But not in my wildest dreams did I think Riley had gotten herself mixed up with this —"

"Diana, I thought you weren't going to say a word."

"I'm not!"

"What are you doing then?"

"Explaining the situation to Kate!"

"Look! We're not going to fight!" yells Daddy.

"We're all going out to dinner together like civilized people, and we're going to have a good time! Now. Where do you want to have dinner?"

"Dinner?" Mom repeats as if she's not familiar with the word.

"Dinner. We're going out to dinner later. Where do you want to go, Kate?"

I'm wondering when are they going to start talking about what's best for me.

"Katie, where to for dinner?"

"Taco Bell."

"Hey, Kate — one more. Over here."

"Mrs. McAllister, how about one with your arms around each other?"

"This way, Cat-Man!"

There are lights and cameras and microphones and people all over the front lawn of Daddy's house.

"Yes," says Daddy for the hundredth time, smiling into a television camera, "she ran away to her grandmother's house."

"And what did you use for transportation, Kate?" asks the reporter, thrusting the microphone at me.

I look at him and say, "Buses. I got there by bus. Three of them."

"Why didn't you contact your parents when they thought you were kidnapped?"

"Scared," says Daddy.

"I was scared," I say.

Daddy's holding my hand and he gives it a little squeeze. I squeeze back. Mom has her arm around me. We all smile at the cameras just like your average, happy family.

"Hey, Cat-Man, let's get one with you standing in the middle."

"This way, Kate!"

"How did you get a bus from Beverly Hills to San Pedro in the middle of the night?" asks a reporter.

"It wasn't easy," says Daddy, and we wave good-bye to the reporters.

"Cat-Man. You've gotta be kidding," says the boy behind the counter at Taco Bell. "It's Cat-Man."

"You know, a lot of people say that," says Daddy. "You really think there's a resemblance?"

"Oh, yeah! You mean you're not Cat-Man? Oh, *yeah*. You could get a job as his double. I mean it."

"You really think so?"

"Any day. That's wild. You look exactly like him. You really should look into getting a job as his double."

"I'll keep that in mind." Daddy turns to Mom and me and asks us what we want to order.

Now the boy is looking at me with a funny, confused sort of expression. "You look familiar, too."

"I'll have a burrito with extra sauce, please," I say.

He writes it down on a chalkboard above the counter. "One burrito."

"Extra sauce. Don't forget the extra sauce."

Mom and Daddy order tacos and Cokes. The air in Taco Bell smells of beans; the tables are brown with orange stripes, and the chairs are yellow, red, blue, and green.

"Are we eating here or in the car?" Mom asks.

"I don't care," says Daddy. "Do you, Katie?"

"No."

"Well, I suppose we better eat in here then," Mom decides. "I know how you hate food smells in your car."

"I do?" Daddy looks surprised.

"Well, you used to."

The boy is getting our order ready but keeps looking over his shoulder at us.

"I don't remember ever saying anything about food smells in my car," says Daddy.

"Kate and I bought dinner at McDonald's once and ate it in your car and you said the car smelled of French fries for weeks."

"I don't remember that at all."

"Water over the dam, Michael." But she's smiling at him.

We get our order on a tray and find a table, which Mom wipes off with a napkin even though there's nothing on it.

"Oh, it isn't cooked." She looks at my burrito as if I've just opened a can of worms. "They're not supposed to look like that, are they?"

I pour on the little carton of extra sauce. "It's cooked, it's just cooked soft."

She sips her Coke. "I've got to tell you both something. I kept waiting for the right time, but maybe there's never a right time." She puts down the Coke and starts to shred her napkin into tiny little pieces. "It's about Chad."

"Chad?" says Daddy."

"My friend Chad."

"Oh, yes . . ."

143

"Well, just before all this business with Kate disappearing — well, Chad asked me to marry him."
Little pieces of napkin float down like snow on the orange-striped table.

My burrito turns to glue inside my mouth. My new stepfather. Chad.

"And?" says Daddy.

"And — I said yes."

"Good. I'm happy for you, Diana."

From the look on his face I can tell he means it. Great. Now they're going to stop fighting and become friends. I call that lousy timing.

17

Now instead of being on a plane going back and forth between the two of them, I'm in a taxi going back and forth between Mom's hotel and Daddy's house. It's the old Ping-Pong ball routine again. Jessica locked herself up in Daddy's den last night when we went to Taco Bell and cried for five hours, so Daddy's decided it's better if Mom doesn't come to the house this weekend. I'm sent out like pizza or Chinese food.

This morning Jessica and Daddy and I sit around the pool. Daddy studies his script, and Jessica keeps oiling her arms and legs. Every once in a while I jump into the pool and do the sidestroke back and forth, then float on my back. What I'm really doing is trying to figure out how to get Mom and Daddy to let me stay with Riley. What I'm afraid of is that when I tell them I want to live with Riley, they'll say "absolutely not," without really considering the idea. And once they say "absolutely not," for some reason they can't change their minds. Mom calls this "sticking to her guns." So I've got to come up with reasons to live with Riley that are so sensible that Mom and Daddy will never have a chance to say "absolutely not."

"Oh, Kate," Jessica says to me as I dry myself off. "I forgot to tell you — Natalie's mother called earlier."

"What did she want?"

"Natalie's back."

I drop my towel and look at her. "Natalie's back? *Why?*"

"Well, Adelle said they didn't want her."

"What? Who didn't want her?"

"Her father and stepmother. They said they didn't have room for her."

"I've got to talk to Natalie! What's their number?"

Her eyebrows go up. "In the address book in the den — I don't understand why you're so upset."

I don't bother to answer her; I fly into the house, find the number, and call Natalie.

Adelle answers. "Who's calling?" she asks.

"Kate McAllister."

There's a long silence, then she says, "Do you understand peer pressure?"

"What?"

"Peer pressure. You know what I'm talking about!"

No wonder Natalie's a little weird. Her mother's crazy, too. "Peer pressure?"

"You talked her into it, didn't you?"

"I hardly know her. I mean — are you talking about her running away to San Diego?"

"What else would I be talking about?"

"I don't know."

"Well, now you know."

"I swear I didn't talk her into it."

Her mother doesn't say anything. Her silence is making me feel guilty. Did I do something to influence Natalie to run away? But she runs away all the time. "May I speak to her, please?"

"Just a minute." The phone clanks down on a table, and after a few minutes, Natalie picks it up.

"I'm so sorry," I say. "What are you going to do?"

"About what?"

"Life."

"What's there to do? *Endure*."

"Come on, Natalie. We're thirteen years old."

"You've got a better idea?"

"Riley's always talking about choices —"

"We're thirteen years old. What choices?"

"Well, the choice to stop feeling sorry for yourself when bad stuff happens and to get on with life —"

"See? *Endure*. Same thing."

I'm feeling so depressed my insides hurt. "How was your brother?"

"Okay. He liked the fish." A pause. "I saw you on the news. You're famous. But don't bite your nails next time you're interviewed. You looked like you were about to swallow your whole hand." Another pause, and then, "Look, don't pay any attention to

147

me. I'm just jealous. You disappear and all of Los Angeles knows about it. I disappear and my mother calls me an ingrate."

"She blamed me. She said I talked you into it."

"Lesson one. Do not believe anything Adelle says. She is under the influence of a very expensive shrink."

"Oh, Natalie." This conversation makes me feel like crying. "Can you come over to my father's house today?"

"I'm grounded. Adelle says she can't trust me. It's the one smart thing she's said all day."

"I've got a new plan I'm working on. I can't talk about it over the phone." Who knows? Maybe Adelle has the phone bugged. "I'll call you back when I work things out."

"I'll be here."

I've just been delivered back to Mom. Daddy and Jessica have to go to a cocktail party, so I'm having dinner with Mom tonight. We walk down Wilshire looking in store windows. Some grown-ups who have problems drink a lot, or jog, or meditate, or take pills. Mom looks in store windows.

We stop in front of a window that's filled with green velvet and one gold chain. "When I talked to Chad today he had some wonderful news," Mom says in a cheerful voice.

If there's anything that makes me more nervous than Mom window-shopping, it's Mom window-shopping *and* sounding cheerful. That's how I know instantly that whatever news Chad had was terrible. "Wonderful news?"

"About a school." She keeps her eyes on the gold chain.

"What about a school?"

"Well, a dear friend of Chad's, who's headmaster of a really marvelous school in Connecticut, has an opening this year. I mean, right now. You could go to boarding school next month." She finally looks at me instead of the gold chain. "What do you think? Isn't that terrific?"

"Boarding school?"

"It's a wonderful place. They have horses and —"

"I don't like horses."

"Of course you do. You just don't have any. You're going to love horses! And the girls have the most darling uniforms —"

"Uniforms?"

"Navy-blue jumpers and white blouses with little Peter Pan collars."

"Yuk!"

"Kate, *try* to be a little more cooperative. This is a very special opportunity."

"It's not special, it stinks! I think it's a lousy opportunity!" But in the middle of my fit I suddenly think: *Mom's right.* Not in the way she means, of course, but this is the opportunity *I've* been waiting for. I continue my fit: "Chad wants to get rid of me. He wants you all to himself!"

Mom looks shocked. "Oh, no, Katie. He doesn't want to get rid of you. This is for your own good."

"He hates me!"

"Oh, *no!*" She gives me a little hug.

I'm not an actor's daughter for nothing. I burst into tears. Mom's so upset she doesn't even notice

149

there's more noise than actual tears. "He's getting rid of me! I'll *die* in boarding school."

People are staring at us. Beverly Hills is not like New York where you could drop dead on the street and nobody would notice. Just get out of your car and *walk* in Beverly Hills and you could get arrested, let alone yell a little bit in the middle of the street.

"Katie, I know it's been a difficult week for you —"

"No, it hasn't been difficult! I had a wonderful time with Riley. I'm sorry you and Daddy got so upset and were worried, but I was happy!"

"Well, I'm glad. I really am glad you were happy, but —"

"But *what?*"

"That's not the point."

"What *is* the point then?"

Mom isn't often at a loss for words. This is like a historical event. She opens her mouth, then closes it, and just looks at me. Finally she hands me a Kleenex, pulls out one for herself, and we start walking slowly back to the hotel.

"I know what would be for my own good," I say.

"What?"

"Living with Riley this year, instead of going to boarding school."

Mom stops in the middle of the sidewalk. "Oh, no . . ." She frowns and shakes her head. "I don't think so, Katie."

But she doesn't say absolutely not.

She starts looking in more store windows and gets a pack of gum out of her purse. I haven't seen her chew gum since she gave up cigarettes and had to

150

chew ten packs of Carefree Sugarless gum every day to stop smoking two packs a day of Virginia Slims. "Besides, your father would never agree to it." She rolls up the gum wrapper and sticks it back in her purse.

"Why not?"

"He's stubborn."

Very carefully, like I'm walking over a mine field, I say, "But he'd realize that he'd see more of me this way. You'd see more of me, too."

Now she's chewing gum like she's doing jaw exercises. "How do you figure that?"

"Well, if I went to boarding school you'd only see me on holidays, right? And you'd have to split up those holidays with Daddy. But this way, since Daddy could see me anytime he wanted at Riley's, you'd have me for *all* the holidays."

She thinks about this for about half a block and then asks, "What have I done wrong?"

"Nothing!"

"I must have done something wrong if you want to live with Riley."

"I want to live with Riley instead of living at boarding school."

"Boarding school is a much healthier environment. You'd be with girls your own age and responsible adults —"

"Riley's house is a very healthy environment! Everybody loves each other and looks out for each other and works together. I mean, how much healthier can you get? They really are a family. And Riley's a responsible adult! She's responsible for Hank and Myra and Fritz and Austin and the garden and

the animals . . ." I run out of breath and feel sus-
pended. There's nothing more I can say.

We walk a whole block without speaking, and
then Mom finally says, "Does what's-his-name still
smell?"

"*Who?*"

"The dog."

"Wagner doesn't smell bad — he just smells like a
dog. And what does that have to do with anything?"

"He's the smelliest dog I've ever met."

I suddenly realize she's run out of objections.
She's going to say yes. Mom's going to let me stay
with Riley.

I think Riley's right. Happy endings belong to
fairy tales. But with a little work and some luck you
might get a good beginning.

Daddy and I watch the red-eye take off for New
York. (He's wearing dark glasses and a baseball cap
so no one will recognize him, but a few people are
staring. Maybe because he's wearing dark glasses at
ten o'clock at night.) To be perfectly honest, there's
a lump in my throat as Mom's plane goes down the
runway, and I had to do my old cool routine of
"see you soon" when I kissed her good-bye. But
Chad's going to be there to meet the plane in New
York, and Mom will be so happy to see him and
busy with plans for the wedding, she won't have time
to feel sad that I'm not with her.

Riley and I are going back for the wedding in
October, and I'll be able to see Shannon then, too.
Daddy's so pleased with our new arrangement that
he offered to come back with us and give the bride

away. Mom thanked him but said it really wasn't necessary.

And I've got a new project to work on: how to get Natalie ungrounded so she can do more birthday parties with us.

We watch Mom's plane, lights flashing, until it disappears into the dark sky. Daddy takes my hand. "Come on, Katie. I've got to get you home to Riley."

It feels like a good beginning.

About the Author

Barbara Abercrombie, a poet and former actress, now spends most of her time writing. Her two teenage daughters, Brooke and Gillan, served as resident critics for *Cat-Man's Daughter,* Ms. Abercrombie's first young adult novel. She is also the author of an adult novel and the editor of an introduction to poetry, which came out of her experiences giving poetry readings and workshops in California elementary schools. Ms. Abercrombie lives with her husband and daughters in Palos Verdes, California.